Finn's Christmas Wish

Ian McEwan 2024

Merry
Christmas

Published by:
Independently published

Merry
Christmas

Table of Contents

Finn and his Christmas Wish

Chapter 1: Finn's Revelation

Finn sat atop a giant, crimson mushroom, his legs dangling over the edge as he stared into the distance. The soft, springy surface beneath him bounced slightly with every fidget, but Finn barely noticed. His thoughts were far away, tangled in a familiar knot. Day after day, it was always the same routine: guard the gold, pull a few tricks, collect a few rewards. Life as a leprechaun wasn't bad, but lately, the shine had dulled.

He scanned the familiar forest around him. The place he'd once thought was full of magic now felt as predictable as the sun rising each morning. Pixies zipped through the air, their wings a blur of silver and gold. A stream gurgled quietly a few yards away, its steady rhythm soothing to most ears. But to Finn, it had become white noise. The air smelled fresh, like moss and pine needles, but even that comforting scent couldn't ease the knot of dissatisfaction in his chest.

"I need something more," Finn muttered under his breath, kicking his feet absently. The words felt heavy, like they'd been stuck inside for too long. He glanced down at his pot of gold, nestled at the base of the mushroom, its coins gleaming in the sunlight. Once, that shine had been enough. When he'd first earned his treasure, each coin had seemed like a symbol of his cunning, his skill in pulling off tricks. He remembered that day—his heart pounding with excitement, the gleam of gold blinding in the afternoon sun. But now? Now, it just seemed hollow.

He sighed and ran a hand through his messy auburn hair. Leprechauns were supposed to be content with their lot, weren't they? A little mischief here, a little gold there—it was the life every young leprechaun aspired to. But something about it all felt too small now, like the world had shrunk around him while his heart was growing, reaching for something more.

The forest around him rustled with life, but Finn barely noticed the usual sights and sounds. The pixies darting through the trees, the faint giggles from the brownies hidden in the moss, the far-off caw of a raven—it all blended into the same background noise he heard every day. What used to be magical now felt ordinary. The same routine, over and over. Was this really all there was?

As if the universe had been listening, a rustling sound broke through the trees. Finn squinted. A figure was approaching, small and quick, weaving through the thick trunks with purpose. It was an elf—a bright, glittering figure, wearing a green uniform adorned with a shiny silver belt and boots. The unmistakable insignia of the North Pole glinted on his chest—a candy cane crossed with a snowflake.

Finn sat up straighter. The North Pole? What would one of Santa's elves be doing this far south?

The elf sauntered over, a jingling bell dangling from the tip of his cap. His grin was wide and confident, and there was something just a little too cheerful about the way he waved.

"Finn O'Malley, right?" the elf called, already too close for Finn's liking.

Finn blinked, caught off guard. "Yeah, that's me," he said slowly, sliding off the mushroom. "And you are?"

"Name's Nibble," the elf said, sticking out a hand with the kind of enthusiasm that made Finn wary. He shook it cautiously, feeling the firm grip of someone who probably had a trick or two up his sleeve. "I'm from Santa's workshop—on a bit of business, you could say."

"Santa's workshop?" Finn asked, curiosity piqued. He'd heard of the place, of course, but leprechauns and elves didn't exactly run in the same circles. "What's that got to do with me?"

"Well, funny you should ask," Nibble said, his grin widening. "We're looking for last-minute recruits. It's toy-making season, and we need all the help we can get."

Finn's heart skipped a beat. Toy-making? The North Pole? Was this the opportunity he'd been hoping for? It was a long shot, sure, but it sounded more exciting than sitting on a pile of gold for the rest of his life. Maybe this was it—his big break.

"You're recruiting? For Santa's workshop?" Finn asked, trying to keep the excitement out of his voice.

Nibble nodded, but there was a flicker of something in his eyes—something calculating. "Yup. Hands are always in short supply this time of year. Elves work hard, but even we need a boost sometimes."

Finn straightened up, eager now. "Well, I've got hands—fast ones! And I'm clever with tools, too. Built a few things myself over the years."

But Nibble chuckled, a short, dismissive sound that instantly made Finn's stomach tighten. "Oh, sure, I'm sure you're handy with your pots of gold," Nibble said, waving his hand like Finn had just made a joke. "But let's be real, this isn't leprechaun work. It's elf business. Different skill set, you know?"

The excitement fizzled in Finn's chest. He frowned, heat rising to his cheeks. "What's that supposed to mean? I'm just as clever as any elf. Maybe more so."

Nibble patted Finn on the shoulder, his grin turning condescending. "Don't take it personally, friend. Leprechauns have their own thing going—gold, tricks, mischief. You're good at what you do. But toys? Christmas cheer? That's elf territory. Not exactly your area of expertise."

Finn's jaw tightened, anger bubbling up inside him. "Who says I can't spread Christmas cheer? Who made up this nonsense about what leprechauns can and can't do?"

Nibble shrugged, jingling the bell on his cap as he turned to leave. "It's not personal. Just the way things are. Good luck with your gold, though!" He gave a mock salute, whistling a merry tune as he disappeared back into the trees.

Finn stood there, fists clenched at his sides. How dare that elf dismiss him like that? Just because he wasn't one of Santa's precious elves didn't mean he couldn't help in the workshop, didn't mean he couldn't bring joy. Leprechauns were clever. Leprechauns were hardworking. Sure, they were prone to tricks now and then, but that didn't mean they couldn't do something meaningful.

"No," Finn muttered under his breath, the anger hardening into determination. "I'm not going to stand for this."

He jumped down from the mushroom and began pacing, frustration surging with every step. Was he really going to let some snobby elves tell him what he was capable of? The words Nibble had thrown at him stung. Gold, tricks, mischief—that's all they thought of leprechauns. But Finn wanted more. Was it so wrong to believe that he could spread cheer, too? That he could do something beyond guarding treasure?

As if on cue, something fluttered past his face, twisting with the wind before drifting toward him. A small, shimmering piece of paper.

He caught it between his fingers. It was a flyer, brightly coloured in red and green, the lettering twinkling like Christmas lights in the sunlight.

Santa's School for Elves!

Train with the best for three months of festive fun. Learn toy-making, sleigh preparation, and Christmas cheer.

Only elves need apply!

Finn's excitement swelled again. A school for Christmas elves? It sounded perfect—a chance to prove himself. Three months of training at the North Pole, surrounded by the magic of the season. But as his eyes fell on the last line, the spark dimmed.

Only elves need apply.

Finn's shoulders slumped. Of course. He wasn't an elf—he was a leprechaun. And leprechauns weren't welcome at Santa's workshop. They were too greedy, too mischievous, too... different.

He crumpled the flyer slightly in his hand, frustration bubbling up again. It wasn't fair. Just because he was a leprechaun didn't mean he didn't have something to offer. Sure, he liked a good prank, but he wasn't greedy, and he certainly wasn't all tricks. He wanted more than just guarding gold and playing the occasional joke. He wanted to make a difference.

"I'm just as capable as any elf," Finn grumbled, straightening his back. "And I'll prove it."

With a new sense of resolve, Finn tucked the flyer into his pocket and marched back toward his burrow. If they wouldn't let him in as a leprechaun, well, maybe he could find a way around that. Leprechauns were known for their cleverness, after all. And if the North Pole wasn't going to give him a chance willingly, he'd just have to make them see what he was made of.

Back in the quiet of his burrow, Finn sat at his small wooden desk, candlelight flickering in the cozy darkness. The scent of damp earth and pine needles filled the room as he stared down at the application form he'd managed to find after hours of searching the village post office. It had been hidden between stacks of letters to Santa—clearly, the elves didn't want leprechauns poking around in their business.

His quill hovered above the parchment, dripping ink as he stared at the blank spaces. He filled out his name quickly:

Finn O'Malley.

Height: Three feet, five inches.

Age: …Well, he wasn't exactly sure about that, so he left it blank. Leprechauns didn't exactly keep track of birthdays.

But when he reached the next section, his quill paused.

Species: Elf?

Finn's fingers tapped nervously on the desk. His mind raced with the consequences. Surely, they didn't need to know everything. He was practically an elf, wasn't he? Small, clever, fast on his feet. How different could they be?

But then doubt crept in. What if they found out? What if, when he showed up, they took one look at him and laughed him out of the workshop? He could almost hear the high-pitched giggles of the elves as they shooed him away, mocking his dreams of something greater.

His stomach twisted. "No," Finn muttered, shaking off the image. He couldn't back out now. He'd come too far. And leprechauns weren't known for quitting, were they?

"It's just a little white lie," he said under his breath. "No harm in that."

With a swift stroke, he scratched down **Elf** in the space provided and chuckled to himself. "No one will even notice."

The rest of the form came easily. Finn listed his skills with gusto:

Toy-making (he'd built plenty of things, though they were mostly traps).
Gift-wrapping (it couldn't be that different from wrapping gold, right?).

Spreading cheer (well, he pulled pranks that made other leprechauns laugh… most of the time).

By the time he finished, he was grinning. "That should do it," he said, sealing the form in an envelope. He marched out into the night, determined to send it off before he could second-guess himself.

As the wind rustled through the trees, carrying the scent of pine and snow, Finn grinned into the darkness. He'd make them see. Whether they liked it or not, Finn O'Malley was going to prove he belonged at the North Pole.

Chapter 2: The Application

Days passed, and Finn's excitement slowly began to morph into impatience. After sending off his application to Santa's School for Elves, he had been checking the mailbox at the end of his cobblestone path every morning, sometimes even twice a day. But it remained empty, save for the occasional wind-blown leaf or scrap of paper.

The first few days had been filled with hope. He would stroll down the path with a spring in his step, humming a tune, already imagining himself at the North Pole, surrounded by elves in their green uniforms, learning the craft of toy-making. But with each passing day, the excitement dulled. Now, instead of a skip in his step, his boots dragged through the dirt, his eyes searching the mailbox with the same question every morning: **Had they forgotten him?**

"Surely they haven't forgotten about me," he muttered one

frosty morning, pacing in front of his burrow. His breath rose in soft clouds around him, the sharp scent of pine cutting through the air. He'd done everything right, hadn't he? Sent the application in good time, filled it out thoroughly (well, mostly). Surely that had to count for something.

The chill in the air nipped at his nose, and Finn tugged his coat tighter around him. The snow had started to dust the tops of the trees, covering the mossy forest floor in a thin layer of white. His pot of gold, which he had recently polished to a gleaming shine, stood beside his door, but even that had lost its luster in his eyes. He'd rearranged every trinket in his cozy home, refitted old traps for fun, and even tried starting a few new projects—but none of it eased the gnawing anticipation.

What if they figured out he wasn't really an elf? The thought crept back, as it always did. What if, as soon as they saw his application, they tossed it aside, laughing at the idea of a leprechaun trying to infiltrate their ranks? His stomach churned at the thought. He could almost hear Nibble's voice in his head, condescending and smug: **"Not elf work, friend. Different skill set."**

"No, no," Finn said aloud, shaking his head and squaring his shoulders. "They wouldn't do that. I've done everything right. I'm just as good as any elf. Better, even!" His voice echoed in the stillness of the forest, but even as he spoke the words, doubt crept in again. He felt it coil in his chest, squeezing tight.

Maybe Nibble had been right after all. Maybe they wouldn't ever accept a leprechaun, no matter how clever or skilled. Maybe elves and leprechauns were just too different, too incompatible. The idea weighed heavy on his heart, pulling him down.

He scuffed at the snow with his boot, frustration bubbling to the surface. All his life, Finn had been clever, quick with his hands and his mind. He had built traps that outwitted other leprechauns, crafted little machines that no one else could figure out. And yet, here he was, waiting like a fool, hoping that some elves—elves!—would take him seriously.

The ticking of the clock inside his burrow seemed louder these days, each tick a reminder of how long he'd been waiting. It had become a companion to his restless pacing, marking the hours and days that slipped by, each one dragging his hopes a little lower. Outside, the wind began to pick up, carrying with it the faint scent of snow. The festive season was well underway, and Finn could hear the faint echoes of carolers from the nearby village, their voices light and merry. It should've made him feel warm, but instead, it only reminded him of how stuck he felt—stuck in the same old routine, the same life he'd always known.

Until one morning, something finally changed.

Finn had almost given up hope. His steps were slower that day as he trudged down the cobblestone path, head bowed against the biting wind. He was ready to turn back, ready to give up the foolish idea of becoming something more. But then, something caught his eye—a flash of red peeking out from the mailbox.

His heart leaped into his throat. Could it be? He rushed forward, barely pausing to lace up his boots, and flung open the mailbox lid.

There it was. A letter.

A bright red envelope, sealed with a glittering green stamp of the North Pole.

For a moment, Finn just stood there, staring at the envelope, hardly daring to believe it. His fingers trembled as he carefully pulled it from the box, feeling the thick, crisp paper between his hands. His breath caught in his throat. This was it. This had to be it.

He looked around, as though expecting someone to tell him it was all a dream, but the forest stood silent. The wind rustled softly through the snow-covered branches, and in the distance, a bird cawed, breaking the stillness. Finn clutched the envelope tighter.

But what if it wasn't good news? What if this was a rejection? What if they'd found out his little white lie? His fingers itched to tear it open, but fear rooted him to the spot. The excitement that had bubbled in his chest was now mixed with a cold dread, swirling in his stomach like a winter storm.

"No," he whispered to himself, shaking his head. "I can't think like that." He had come too far, worked too hard to let doubt creep in now. Whatever was in that letter, he had to face it.

With trembling hands, Finn tore open the envelope, his eyes scanning the page inside. For a moment, the words blurred together, and he had to blink twice to make sure he was reading them right.

Dear Finn O'Malley,

Congratulations! You've been accepted to Santa's School for

Merry
Christmas

Elves.

We look forward to seeing you at the North Pole for three months of intensive training.

Finn's heart raced. He read the lines over again, just to be sure. There it was—**Congratulations. Accepted.** His hands trembled as he clutched the letter tighter. He could hardly believe it. They had accepted him! He was going to the North Pole. He—a leprechaun—was about to train with the very best, right alongside Santa's elite elves.

A grin split across his face, wide and uncontainable. He let out a shout of pure joy, punching the air. This was more than he had hoped for. It wasn't just about leaving behind the mundane life of guarding gold—it was about proving himself. Leprechauns weren't just tricksters. They were clever, determined, resourceful. And now, finally, Finn was going to show the world what he was capable of.

But then, his eyes caught on one last line at the bottom of the letter, and his grin faltered.

Please bring this letter with you for verification upon arrival.

Verification.

Finn's fingers tightened around the paper. Of course, they'd want to verify his identity. They'd be expecting an elf to show up. His pulse quickened, and for a moment, panic bubbled up in his chest. What if they saw through him the moment he stepped off the sleigh bus? What if they discovered he wasn't who he said he was?

Images flashed through his mind—elves with narrowed eyes,

pointing fingers, laughter ringing in his ears as they escorted him out of the North Pole. The thought made his stomach twist.

But then, just as quickly, Finn shook his head, banishing the fear. He had made it this far. A little magic, a little cleverness, and he could keep up the act. He'd been pulling tricks his whole life. Surely, he could fool a few elves for three months. And if he proved himself during training, they wouldn't care what species he was. **Talent was talent**, and Finn had plenty of that.

"I'll make them see," Finn muttered under his breath. "I'll show them that I belong."

He folded the letter carefully, tucking it into his coat pocket. The weight of it felt both comforting and daunting at the same time. But Finn straightened his shoulders, determination settling in his chest like a warm flame. He'd find a way to pull this off. He always did.

And whether the North Pole liked it or not, Finn O'Malley was going to prove that he belonged there.

Chapter 3: The Journey to Elf School

The journey to the North Pole was nothing short of magical.

For most of Finn's life, his world had been a small, moss-covered patch of Ireland, nestled in a quiet corner of the forest where the trees grew thick and the sunlight rarely broke through the canopy. But now, as he gazed out from the sleigh bus, that world seemed impossibly far away. Before him

Merry
Christmas

stretched a vast expanse of white—snow-covered mountains that loomed in the distance like ancient sentinels, their peaks lost in a swirl of mist. Below, frozen lakes glistened under the pale moonlight, reflecting the shimmering northern lights that danced across the sky like ribbons of color. Towering pine forests blanketed in snow spread out beneath him, the trees standing silent and majestic, their branches heavy with icicles.

Finn had never seen anything like it. His breath caught in his throat, his heart swelling with a mix of awe and disbelief. He'd heard stories about places like this—distant lands full of magic and wonder—but to see it with his own eyes felt almost unreal.

The sleigh bus—a massive, red and gold sleigh powered by a team of reindeer—swooped through the air, leaving glittering trails of stardust in its wake. The reins jingled in time with the rhythm of the reindeer's hooves, and every now and then, a burst of magic sparked in the air, sending tiny snowflakes cascading around them like glittering diamonds. The wind rushed past, cold and biting, nipping at Finn's cheeks and making his auburn hair whip around his face. He clutched his bag tightly, pulling his coat tighter against the chill as he sat near the back, surrounded by other elves. Their chatter filled the air with a bubbling excitement that Finn couldn't quite share, though he wished he could.

He kept his head down, doing his best to blend in. The last thing he needed was attention. So far, he had managed to pass himself off as just another recruit—none of the elves seemed to suspect that there was a leprechaun in their midst. But as the sleigh bus soared through the night sky, the weight of the upcoming challenge settled heavily on his shoulders, a weight he hadn't quite anticipated. He was about to walk into Santa's School for Elves, one of the most prestigious institutions in the magical world, and he was doing it under false pretenses.

Finn's stomach twisted, and he cast a quick glance around at the other elves. They were all chatting excitedly, their faces lit up with enthusiasm, their hands gesturing as they talked about the school, the classes, the training they were about to receive. They all seemed so... certain. So confident in their place here. It made Finn feel even more like an outsider, like a fraud. **What if someone recognized he wasn't really an elf?** His fingers brushed against the envelope tucked inside his coat pocket—the letter that had brought him here, the letter that carried the weight of his lie. "Verification upon arrival." That phrase had been haunting him since the moment he'd read it, twisting his stomach into tighter knots with every passing mile.

He took a shaky breath and closed his eyes for a moment, trying to calm the rising tide of anxiety. **I just need to blend in.** He repeated it like a mantra, as if saying it enough times would make it true. **As long as I don't do anything to stand out, I'll be fine. I'll make it through training, and they'll never know.**

But even as he told himself that, doubt gnawed at the back of his mind. What if someone asked too many questions? What if the elves noticed something different about him, something that set him apart? Leprechauns were known for their tricks and mischief, not for spreading Christmas cheer or building toys. Could he really pull this off?

The sleigh bus jolted slightly, pulling him from his thoughts as they began to descend. The icy landscape of the North Pole sprawled out beneath them, vast and glittering under the pale morning light. Finn's breath caught in his throat again, but this time it wasn't just from the cold.

Below them, snow-covered buildings twinkled with colorful lights, their roofs adorned with strands of sparkling tinsel. Winding paths carved through the snow like ribbons of white, connecting the buildings to one another, and in the distance, towering over everything else, were the spires of Santa's School for Elves. The school looked like something out of a fairy tale—its towering spires stretched toward the sky, disappearing into the swirling clouds above, while its windows glowed with a warm, golden light. Snowflakes drifted lazily around the towers, catching the light and making the entire scene look as though it had been dipped in stardust.

Finn stared, wide-eyed, taking it all in. It was more magical than he'd ever imagined. For a moment, all his fears were forgotten, swept away by the sheer wonder of the sight before him. **This was the North Pole.** This was the place where magic was made, where joy and wonder were crafted and sent out into the world.

But then, the sleigh bus touched down on a wide, snowy platform with a soft thud, and reality came rushing back. The reindeer snorted clouds of frost into the cold air, shaking their antlers as the sleigh came to a stop. The elves around Finn scrambled to their feet, chattering excitedly as they grabbed their bags and made their way toward the towering entrance of the school.

Finn hesitated for a moment, his heart thudding in his chest.

This was it. There was no turning back now. He took a deep breath, hoisted his bag over his shoulder, and stepped off the sleigh.

The platform buzzed with activity. Elves hurried about, their breath rising in little puffs of steam as they called out instructions and waved new recruits forward. Each of them clutched letters similar to Finn's, and the air hummed with anticipation. Snow crunched underfoot as the recruits made their way toward the entrance, where a stern-looking elf with a clipboard stood, checking names and verifying identities.

Finn's heart skipped a beat. **Verification.** His hand instinctively went to the envelope in his pocket, and he felt a surge of panic rise in his chest. What if they looked at him too closely? What if they noticed something was off? He swallowed hard and tried to push the fear down, telling himself again and again that everything would be fine.

He joined the line of eager recruits, his hands trembling slightly as he clutched the letter tighter. The stern elf checked off names one by one, barely glancing up as each recruit handed over their letter. Every few seconds, the elf would glance at each newcomer, give a curt nod, and wave them through.

Finn was next.

"Name?" the stern elf asked, without looking up from his clipboard.

"Finn O'Malley," Finn said, trying to sound confident, though his voice wavered ever so slightly.

The elf flipped through the pages of his list, his brow furrowing for a moment as he scanned the names. Finn's heart pounded in his chest. **What if his name wasn't there?** What if the application had been flagged? The seconds stretched out, each one feeling like an eternity.

But then, with a curt nod, the elf checked off his name. "You're on the list. Welcome to Santa's School for Elves. Verification?"

Finn handed over the letter with a shaky hand, hoping his nerves didn't show. The elf took it, glanced over the contents briefly, and then handed it back with little fanfare.

"Everything seems to be in order. Proceed inside."

Finn exhaled, the breath he hadn't realized he'd been holding escaping in a rush of relief. **He had made it.** He was in.

As he stepped through the towering entrance and into the grand halls of Santa's School for Elves, the nerves that had been gnawing at him began to fade, replaced by something else—excitement. The interior of the school was even more breathtaking than he had imagined. The high ceilings were draped with garlands of holly and ivy, and twinkling lights floated in the air like little stars. The walls shimmered with magic, casting a warm, golden glow over everything.

For the first time since he'd set out on this journey, Finn allowed himself to relax—just a little. He had made it through the first hurdle. He was really here.

And now, he was one step closer to proving that he belonged.

Chapter 4: Elf School Begins

The inside of Santa's School for Elves was more magical than Finn could have ever imagined. Glittering icicles draped the grand staircases, glowing softly with an ethereal light. Holly and mistletoe hung in every corner, and the smell of fresh gingerbread and peppermint filled the air. Elves bustled about, some carrying stacks of presents, others adjusting garlands or hanging baubles that twinkled like stars. Everything seemed to shimmer with the spirit of Christmas.

Finn stood in the main hall, taking it all in, his breath caught in his chest. This was the North Pole. This was where magic happened. He couldn't believe he was really here.

But the moment of awe didn't last long. A voice boomed through the hall, calling all new recruits to gather in the courtyard for orientation. Finn quickly followed the crowd of elves, his heart thudding with a mix of excitement and nerves.

In the courtyard, the head instructor—an older, stern-looking elf named Master Evergreen—stood on a platform, clipboard in hand. His sharp eyes scanned the crowd, and when he spoke, his voice was crisp and authoritative.

"Welcome to Santa's School for Elves," Master Evergreen began, his gaze sweeping over the recruits. "You have been chosen to train here because you possess qualities, we look for in the elves who help keep Christmas running smoothly—intelligence, creativity, teamwork. Over the next three months, you will be tested in ways you cannot yet imagine. Toy-making, sleigh preparation, holiday cheer—it all requires dedication and skill. Not everyone here will make it to the end. Only the best will move on to work in Santa's workshop."

Finn swallowed hard. This was going to be even more challenging than he'd thought.

Master Evergreen continued, explaining that the recruits would be divided into dormitories, each group representing one of Santa's reindeer. Finn found himself in Dormitory 17, along with a group of elves he hadn't met before. As he scanned the list, he found his name paired with another elf—Elmer Brightspark.

Just then, a bright-eyed, curly-haired elf bounced over to Finn, a wide grin on his face.

"Hey! You must be Finn!" the elf said enthusiastically, offering his hand. "I'm Elmer Brightspark! We're bunkmates. This is going to be great!"

Finn shook his hand, smiling despite his nerves. "Yeah, I guess it is."

As the new recruits were led to their dormitories, Finn's mind raced with thoughts of what was to come. He had made it this far, but the real challenge was just beginning.

He'd have to be smart. Careful. But more than anything, he'd have to prove to everyone here—especially himself—that he could do it.

He wasn't just a leprechaun. He was Finn O'Malley, and he was going to make his mark on Christmas.

Chapter 5: The First Day of Training

The inside of Santa's School for Elves was more magical than Finn could have ever imagined.

As he stepped through the grand entrance, his breath caught in his chest. The hall before him was a dazzling display of holiday cheer brought to life. Glittering icicles draped the towering staircases, glowing softly with an ethereal light that seemed to come from within the ice itself. Each icicle shimmered with hues of blue, white, and silver, casting dancing reflections on the polished marble floors. Holly and mistletoe hung in every corner, their deep green leaves glossy and vibrant, dotted with bright red berries that seemed to sparkle as though kissed by magic. The air was rich with the scent of fresh gingerbread, peppermint, and hot cocoa—a warm, comforting smell that wrapped around Finn like a hug.

Elves bustled about, their small forms a blur of green and red as they hurried to and fro, some carrying stacks of presents wrapped in brightly colored paper, others adjusting garlands or hanging baubles that twinkled like tiny stars suspended in midair. Laughter and soft conversation floated through the air, mingling with the faint jingling of bells and the occasional burst of Christmas carols. Everything here seemed to shimmer with the spirit of Christmas, as though the very walls were infused with magic.

Even the floors glowed with a soft golden hue, like they had been dusted with stardust. The light reflected off the marble in delicate patterns, giving the whole hall an almost otherworldly quality, as though Finn had stepped into a dream.

Finn stood in the main hall, wide-eyed, drinking in every detail. **This was the North Pole.** This was where the magic of Christmas was made, where joy was crafted by hand and sent out to the world. **And he was standing right in the middle of it.**

For a brief moment, all the doubts that had been gnawing at him melted away, leaving only awe. His chest swelled with excitement, his heart pounding against his ribs. **This is what I've been waiting for,** he thought, barely able to contain the grin threatening to spread across his face. **I made it. I'm really here.**

But the moment of wonder didn't last long.

A voice boomed through the hall, shattering the spell of the moment. "All new recruits, gather in the courtyard for orientation!"

Finn blinked, the sudden sound jolting him out of his reverie. Around him, the other recruits had already started moving, a stream of eager elves hurrying toward the courtyard doors. Finn quickly fell in line behind them, his heart thudding with a mix of excitement and nerves. The butterflies in his stomach were back, swirling like a storm. **This is it,** he thought. **No turning back now.**

As they stepped outside into the frosty courtyard, Finn's breath puffed out in soft clouds, mingling with the crisp, cold air. Snow covered the ground, its surface glittering under the soft glow of lanterns strung along the courtyard walls. The cold bit at his cheeks, and he pulled his coat tighter around him, though the chill barely registered. His attention was fixed on the figure standing on a raised platform in the center of the courtyard.

It was an older elf, tall and stern, with a presence that commanded attention. His sharp gaze seemed to cut through the crowd like a blade, missing nothing. His silver hair was tied back in a neat bun, and his green cloak was fastened with a golden clasp shaped like a snowflake. In one hand, he held a large brass bell, which he rang once. The sound echoed through the courtyard, sharp and clear, bringing all conversation to an abrupt halt.

"Welcome to Santa's School for Elves," the elf announced, his voice crisp and authoritative. His sharp eyes swept over the crowd, lingering on each recruit for just a moment before moving on, as though he could measure their worth with a single glance. "I am Master Evergreen, head instructor. You have been chosen to train here because you possess the qualities we look for in the elves who help keep Christmas running smoothly—intelligence, creativity, and teamwork."

Finn swallowed hard, feeling a lump form in his throat. **Chosen,** he repeated in his mind, the word echoing like a bell. **Was he really chosen?** Or had he just slipped in by accident—a trickster leprechaun pretending to belong? His heart raced as he glanced around at the other recruits. They stood tall and eager, their faces shining with pride and determination. None of them had to hide who they were.

For a moment, Finn felt like a shadow among them.

Master Evergreen's voice cut through his thoughts like a knife. "Over the next three months, you will be tested in ways you cannot yet imagine. Toy-making, sleigh preparation, holiday cheer—it all requires dedication and skill. Not everyone here will make it to the end. Only the best will move on to work in Santa's workshop."

Finn's stomach flipped. **Not everyone will make it?** His pulse quickened, his breath coming a little shorter. The excitement that had been bubbling inside him just moments ago suddenly felt less like anticipation and more like pressure. He had known this would be hard, but hearing it laid out like this made it feel... real. **Could he really compete with the elves?** Could he pass their tests? **What if someone found out? What if they didn't even let him finish once they knew the truth?**

He glanced down at his hands, realizing they were shaking. He stuffed them into his coat pockets, trying to calm the rising tide of anxiety threatening to overwhelm him. **You can do this,** he told himself. **Just stay focused.**

Master Evergreen continued, his tone firm and unyielding. "You will be assigned to dormitories, each named after one of Santa's reindeer. This will be your home for the duration of your training. You will work together, study together, and succeed—or fail—together."

Finn's breath hitched. **Fail?** The word sent a shiver down his spine. **Failure wasn't an option.** He had left everything behind to be here. He had lied to get here. And now, he had to prove that he was worthy of the place he had stolen. There was no going back.

When the names were called, Finn barely heard them. His

mind was too busy racing with thoughts of the challenges ahead, of the tests he'd have to pass, and the eyes that would be watching his every move. **Everything was on the line.**

It was only when he heard his name that he snapped back to reality.

"Finn O'Malley—Dormitory 17, with Elmer Brightspark."

Finn scanned the crowd, looking for his new dormmate. His heart pounded in his chest. He hadn't met any of the other recruits yet, and the sea of unfamiliar faces made his pulse quicken even more. **Who was Elmer Brightspark?** Was he like Master Evergreen—stern and intense? Would he be suspicious of Finn?

Just then, a bright-eyed, curly-haired elf bounced over to him, grinning from ear to ear. His cheeks were flushed pink from the cold, and there was an infectious energy about him that made Finn's nerves soften, if only a little.

"Hey! You must be Finn!" the elf said enthusiastically, sticking out his hand. "I'm Elmer Brightspark! We're bunkmates. This is going to be great!"

Elmer's energy was overwhelming, but not in a bad way. It was warm, almost comforting—like a burst of sunlight on a cold day. Finn shook his hand, trying to muster up a smile despite the swirl of nerves still churning in his chest. "Yeah, I guess it is," he said, his voice a little shakier than he'd have liked.

As the recruits were led toward their dormitories, Finn's mind buzzed with thoughts of what was to come. The school felt massive, like a sprawling maze of holiday wonder. Twinkling lights lined the corridors, casting a soft, warm glow over everything, and each window framed a perfect view of the snow falling gently outside. He could hear the soft hum of Christmas carols echoing through the halls, mingling with the occasional clatter of elves hard at work in other parts of the building. It

was enchanting—but also overwhelming.

The sheer scale of the school pressed down on Finn as he walked, making him feel small and out of place. He glanced around at the other recruits, most of whom seemed to be taking everything in stride, chatting easily as they followed their assigned dormmates. Elmer was practically bouncing with excitement, his energy never wavering. Finn, on the other hand, felt the weight of every step. **How does he do it?** Finn wondered. How could Elmer manage to be so confident, so carefree in a place like this, with so much at stake?

Finn tried to mirror Elmer's enthusiasm, but doubt nagged at the edges of his mind. **What if he made a mistake?** What if he slipped up during training and exposed himself as the imposter he feared he was? The eyes of the instructors would be on him, watching for any sign of weakness, any hint that he didn't belong. He couldn't afford a single misstep.

As they reached Dormitory 17, Finn took a deep breath, trying to steady his nerves. The building was cozy, its wooden beams wrapped in garlands of holly and pine, twinkling fairy lights strung along the walls. A large fireplace crackled at the far end of the common room, its flames casting a warm, orange glow over the space. There were comfortable chairs arranged in clusters, and shelves stacked with books on toy-making, sleigh engineering, and Christmas magic. A large window overlooked

the snow-covered courtyard, offering a breathtaking view of
the swirling snowflakes outside.

For a moment, the warmth of the room wrapped around Finn
like a blanket, soothing the cold anxiety gnawing at his insides. **Maybe this won't be so bad,** he thought. The dormitory
felt safe, like a retreat from the pressures of the school. It was
a place where he could catch his breath, regroup, and prepare
for whatever challenges lay ahead.

Elmer bounced over to one of the bunk beds, tossing his bag
onto the lower bunk with a grin. "I call bottom bunk!" he
announced cheerfully, as though it were the greatest victory in
the world.

Finn couldn't help but chuckle. "Fine by me," he said, his voice
more relaxed than it had been all day. He slung his own bag
onto the top bunk, feeling a bit of the tension melt away.

Elmer turned to him, his eyes sparkling with excitement. "I
can't believe we're actually here, can you? I've been dream-
ing about this for ages! The toy-making workshops, the sleigh
flights, learning from Master Evergreen—it's going to be amazing!" He spoke so quickly that Finn could barely keep up, but
the enthusiasm was infectious.

"Yeah," Finn said, nodding. "It's pretty amazing." His voice was
steady, but inside, a storm of uncertainty still brewed. **Would
it still feel amazing once the training started?** Could he really
keep up with all the elves, especially when so much was riding
on him not being found out?

Elmer didn't seem to notice Finn's hesitation. He plopped
down on the edge of the bed, bouncing slightly on the mat-

tress, his eyes full of wonder. "I can't wait to get started," he said, almost to himself. "We're going to learn so much. This is our big chance, Finn! Our chance to be part of something really special."

Finn smiled, though it didn't quite reach his eyes. **Elmer didn't know how different their situations were.** For him, this was a dream come true—a chance to be the best, to join Santa's elite team of elves. But for Finn, this was about survival. It wasn't just a chance to prove himself; it was his only chance.

He took a deep breath, his gaze falling on the crackling fire in the hearth. He had made it this far, but the real challenge was just beginning. Tomorrow, the tests would start—tests he had to pass, no matter what. Every move he made would be scrutinized. Every mistake could bring him one step closer to being discovered. And failure? **Failure wasn't an option.**

But more than anything, Finn had to prove to himself—and to everyone else—that he could do it. That he wasn't just a trickster leprechaun who had bluffed his way in. He had to prove that he deserved to be here, even if he wasn't like the others. **Even if he wasn't an elf.**

As Finn opened the door to their shared room, the warmth of the dormitory washed over him once more, and for the first time since he'd arrived, he allowed himself a small, cautious smile.

I can do this.

He wasn't just a leprechaun. He was Finn O'Malley, and he was going to make his mark on Christmas

Chapter 6: Secrets and Sleds

The next few days passed in a blur of activity.

Santa's School for Elves moved at a pace Finn hadn't antici-pated—fast and relentless. From the moment the first golden rays of dawn streamed through the frosted windows, the new recruits were swept into a whirlwind of tasks that carried them well past dusk. The schedule was packed with toy-making, sleigh preparation, and lessons on holiday cheer. There was barely time to catch his breath between classes, let alone pro-cess everything that was happening.

Finn did his best to keep up, to blend in with the elves, but there were moments—small but significant—when he felt the weight of his secret pressing down on him, threatening to suffocate the joy he so desperately wanted to feel.

The toy-making workshops were the hardest. The elves around him moved with a fluid grace that came from years of practice, their nimble fingers expertly twisting, hammering, and shaping toys with precision and care. Finn had thought himself clever with his hands—after all, he'd built plenty of traps and devic-es back home—but the intricacies of elf craftsmanship were on another level entirely. Each toy seemed to have a touch of magic woven into its design, and Finn's clumsy efforts felt heavy and awkward by comparison.

And then there were the tools.

The sleigh-making workshops introduced him to a dizzying ar-ray of unfamiliar instruments: wrenches, clamps, and enchant-ed hammers that shimmered faintly with magic. Finn's hands, usually so sure, fumbled with them like a child playing with his first set of blocks. The first few lessons passed in tense silence as he struggled to imitate the elves around him, but it wasn't long before his awkwardness drew attention.

It was during one of these workshops, while assembling a sleigh's frame, that Finn felt a pair of eyes on him. The hairs on the back of his neck prickled. He glanced up from the stubborn bolt he'd been wrestling with and met the sharp gaze of Kieran, a tall, dark-haired elf who had been assigned to the same workshop group.

Kieran was watching him with a look that made Finn's heart skip a beat. There was nothing outwardly suspicious in the elf's demeanor, but there was something about the way he always seemed to hover near Finn, his eyes a little too observant, his questions a little too casual.

"You alright there, Finn?" Kieran asked, his voice light, but his gaze unwavering.

Finn's fingers slipped on the wrench, and he forced a smile, tightening a screw that didn't really need tightening. "Yeah, just getting the hang of it," he said, trying to sound casual.

Kieran's brow lifted slightly, and though he didn't say anything more, Finn could feel the weight of his attention. It was as if Kieran could sense that something wasn't quite right—that Finn didn't belong, even if he couldn't put his finger on it yet.

For the rest of the lesson, Finn worked in silence, focusing on each bolt, each tool, as though his life depended on it. But no matter how hard he tried, he couldn't shake the feeling that Kieran was seeing more than Finn wanted him to.

As the days wore on, Finn found himself caught in a delicate balancing act. The pressure mounted, and each new task seemed like another opportunity for his secret to slip out. In the toy-making classes, he copied the elves around him as best he could, watching their techniques with careful eyes, but every mistake—every misplaced part or misaligned seam—felt like it was magnified tenfold. In the sleigh workshops, the intricate mechanics and enchanted tools required precision that Finn had to force himself to mimic, his hands stiff and unsure.

The elves seemed to sense something was off, though none of them voiced it directly. There were moments when Finn caught lingering glances, a raised eyebrow here, a shared look there. Kieran, in particular, seemed to hover nearby more often than was necessary, always offering a word of advice or asking a question that felt a little too pointed.

The elves were friendly—almost too friendly—and that was part of what made it so hard. Finn liked them. He didn't want to deceive them. But he had no choice. He wasn't like the others. **He wasn't an elf.** And sooner or later, someone was going to figure it out.

Every night, as he lay in his bunk, Finn's thoughts swirled like a blizzard. His mind raced through the day's events, picking apart every interaction, every misstep. **How long before someone realized he didn't belong?** He had slipped into this world with a lie, and it was only a matter of time before that lie unraveled.

But he couldn't leave. Not now. Not after everything.

Every time the doubt threatened to take over, every time

he felt like giving up and running back to his quiet burrow in Ireland, he reminded himself of why he was here. He wanted more than the life he had left behind. He wanted to be part of something bigger, something meaningful. This was his chance to prove that he could do more than just guard a pot of gold and pull pranks. **This was his chance to be someone.**

And so, he stayed. He played the part. He laughed when the others laughed, worked when the others worked, and kept his head down when the pressure became too much.

One evening, after a particularly grueling sleigh-preparation session, Elmer Brightspark—Finn's ever-enthusiastic bunk-mate—plopped down beside him in the dorm common area, his cheeks flushed from the cold, his curly hair sticking out in all directions.

"Whew! That was tough, huh?" Elmer grinned, wiping the sweat from his brow. "Who knew making sleighs was such hard work?"

Finn forced a laugh, his hands still aching from the day's efforts. "Yeah, tough is one way to put it."

Elmer didn't seem to notice the weariness in Finn's voice. He was already off on one of his endless tangents, babbling excitedly about tomorrow's toy-making challenge and how he was sure they'd be building some sort of mechanical train set. Finn nodded along, trying to muster up the same excitement, but all he could think about was the growing weight of his secret.

Elmer was nice—more than nice, really. He was a ball of energy and optimism, the kind of person who made everything seem possible. But Finn couldn't help but feel guilty every time Elmer smiled at him. **What would Elmer think if he found out?** Would he see Finn as a fraud? Would he look at him the way Kieran did, with suspicion lurking behind every glance?

Finn shook off the thought, pulling himself back into the present. He couldn't afford to get lost in worry. Not now.

The next few days would be even more challenging, and Finn needed to stay sharp. **One wrong move, and it could all come crashing down.**

But for now, he'd keep playing the part.

Chapter 7: Trouble in the Team

By the second week of training, the recruits had begun to settle into a rhythm.

Each day was packed with lessons, physical challenges, and team-building exercises designed to test not only their skills but their ability to work together under pressure. For Finn, every day was a delicate dance—he was working harder than he ever had before, his muscles aching from the physical demands, but his mind raced constantly, weighed down by the pressure to fit in. Every task felt like a trial. Not just of his skills, but of his ability to keep his secret hidden.

His dormitory group—Team Donner—had begun to gel, at least on the surface. The elves worked together well enough, but beneath the teamwork, Finn could feel cracks forming. He got along well with Elmer, whose cheerful personality made the long days more bearable, and Brigid, with her quiet, calming presence, often stepped in to ease the tension when things got heated. But Kieran Shadowbrook, with his sharp-eyed gaze and quiet intensity, was proving more difficult.

It wasn't that Kieran was outright rude or dismissive—he was just... watchful. He moved with a quiet confidence, skilled and precise, rarely making mistakes, but there was an air of superiority about him that rubbed Finn the wrong way. It was the way Kieran looked at him, like he was always on the verge of seeing something that Finn didn't want him to see. Finn couldn't shake the feeling that Kieran was evaluating him, scrutinizing his every move, just waiting for something to slip.

But Kieran wasn't the only source of tension.

Another elf in their group, Nessa Goldenbloom, had a habit of taking charge at every opportunity. Tall and commanding, with golden curls and a sharp tongue, Nessa was quick to point out flaws in everyone's work and seemed to thrive on controlling the situation. Finn had learned to bite his tongue around her— Nessa didn't like being questioned, and it wasn't worth the argument. But her bossy nature was starting to wear on the rest of the group.

By the time the **Sleigh-Building Challenge** arrived, the strain was already starting to show.

The Sleigh-Building Challenge

The recruits gathered in the snowy courtyard, their breaths visible in the cold air. The sky above was a thick blanket of gray, the clouds hanging low as though the weight of the coming snow pressed down on the earth. Finn pulled his coat tighter around him, feeling the cold bite at his cheeks and ears. He could sense the tension crackling in the air—today was important, and everyone knew it.

Master Evergreen stood at the front of the courtyard, his stern gaze sweeping over the assembled teams. His green cloak billowed slightly in the wind, and his silver hair gleamed under the dull light of the sky. Behind him, a large sleigh stood as a shining example, painted a festive red with gold trim that shimmered even under the overcast sky. A row of tools and neatly stacked wooden planks lay in front of each team's workstation, ready to be transformed into functional sleighs.

"This challenge," Master Evergreen began, his voice crisp and sharp as the winter air, "will test not only your craftsmanship but your ability to work as a team. Each group will be tasked with building a sleigh—strong, sturdy, and capable of carrying a load. You will need to assemble it from scratch, following the provided instructions." He paused, letting the weight of the task settle over them.

"But," he continued, "this is not just about who can finish first. The quality of your sleigh will be judged on its construction, creativity, and durability. You have four hours. Begin."

The courtyard erupted into action as the teams rushed to their stations, voices overlapping as they strategized. Team Donner gathered around their pile of supplies, the air already thick with the unspoken tension that had been building all week.

"Okay," Kieran said, stepping up to take the lead, as he always did. "We need to get the frame sorted first. If we don't get the base right, the whole thing will collapse."

Finn grabbed a wrench, eager to contribute. He still felt the constant need to prove himself, to show the others that he could handle this—especially Kieran. "I'll handle the bolts," he said quickly, hoping his confidence didn't sound forced.

But before he could get started, Nessa Goldenbloom cut in, her voice sharp and decisive. "No, I'll handle the bolts," she said, already reaching for the tools. "This is about precision, Finn, and we don't have time for mistakes."

Finn's jaw tightened, the sting of her words hitting harder than he wanted to admit. **I haven't made any mistakes yet,** he thought bitterly, but Nessa acted like he was a ticking time bomb, ready to blow any moment.

"Why don't we all just focus on what we're good at?" Elmer piped up, ever the peacemaker. He flashed Finn an encouraging smile. "Finn, you've been great with tools so far. Kieran can handle the frame, and Brigid, you're good with details—maybe you could help with the measurements?"

Brigid nodded, offering a small smile, but Nessa wasn't having it. She folded her arms, her golden curls bouncing as she shook her head. "This isn't about everyone doing what they're 'good at,' Elmer. It's about efficiency. We don't have time for everyone to take turns experimenting."

Finn could feel the heat rising in his chest. **Experimenting?** He wasn't experimenting—he knew what he was doing. But arguing with Nessa was pointless. She always had to be right, always had to be in control.

Instead, he took a deep breath and focused on the task at hand. The hours ticked by in tense silence, broken only by the occasional barked order from Kieran or a sharp comment from Nessa. The sleigh slowly began to take shape—its frame sturdy, the wood polished to a fine sheen. But with each passing minute, the tension grew thicker, weighing down the group like a heavy blanket.

It all came to a head when they were almost done. The frame was nearly complete, the final touches being added. But as Finn watched Nessa tighten the bolts on the joints, something didn't look right.

"The joints are too tight," Finn said, trying to keep his voice steady. He pointed to where the wooden beams were creaking under the pressure. "If we don't loosen them a bit, the whole frame could collapse under the weight."

Nessa shot him a withering look, her eyes narrowing in irritation. "I know what I'm doing, Finn. I've built sleighs before."

"I'm just saying—" Finn began, but Nessa cut him off, her voice snapping like a whip.

"Stop questioning everything!" she snapped. "You're not in charge here. I am."

Finn's frustration bubbled over. He had been biting his tongue all day, but Nessa's arrogance was too much. "This isn't about being in charge—it's about doing the job right! You're going to break it if you keep tightening those bolts!"

Before the argument could escalate further, Kieran stepped in, his voice cold and sharp. "Enough. Finn's right. The joints are too tight."

For a moment, Nessa looked like she might argue, but then she stepped back, her lips pressed into a thin line. "Fine. Do it your way."

Finn quickly loosened the bolts, adjusting the joints until the frame was more secure. The sleigh still looked strong, its red paint gleaming in the fading light, but there was no sense of accomplishment. No shared feeling of success. The group stood in silence, the strain of the day hanging heavily between them like a dark cloud.

The Aftermath

After the challenge, the recruits were given the afternoon off to rest and prepare for the next day, but Finn couldn't shake the frustration that had built up during the sleigh-building task. His chest was tight with the lingering tension, his thoughts swirling like the snowflakes that drifted lazily through the air. He wandered the grounds, the cold wind biting at his cheeks, replaying the argument with Nessa over and over in his mind.

He didn't like confrontation. He had spent most of his life avoiding it, preferring to keep his head down and stay out of trouble. But Nessa's arrogance had pushed him too far. **She wasn't just difficult—she was jeopardizing the team's chances of success.** And Finn couldn't afford to let that happen. Not when everything was riding on these challenges.

As he walked along the snow-covered paths, Finn heard the crunch of footsteps behind him. He turned to see Kieran approaching, his dark eyes unreadable.

"Hey," Kieran said, his voice flat and unreadable.

"Hey," Finn replied, bracing himself for whatever Kieran was about to say.

For a moment, Kieran didn't speak. He just stood there, watching Finn with that same sharp gaze that always made him feel exposed, vulnerable. Finally, Kieran crossed his arms, letting out a breath that formed a small cloud in the frigid air.

"You were right," Kieran said, his voice low but firm. "About the sleigh. If you hadn't spoken up, it would've collapsed."

Finn blinked, caught off guard. "I—thanks. I just didn't want to see it fall apart."

Kieran nodded, his expression softening slightly. "Look, I know Nessa's difficult. She wants to be in charge, and she doesn't like being questioned. But she's good at what she does. We just... need to figure out how to work with her."

Finn's frustration bubbled up again. "It's not just about working with her. She doesn't listen to anyone else. It's like she thinks she knows everything."

Kieran was quiet for a moment, then gave a small shrug. "She's got her reasons, I guess. But we can't let this kind of thing get in the way. The challenges are only going to get harder. We need to figure out how to work as a team."

Finn sighed, running a hand through his hair. He knew Kieran was right, but that didn't make it any easier. "I just don't get it. We're all here to do the same thing—prove ourselves. Why does it have to be so hard?"

Kieran gave him a long, measured look. "Because everyone's got something to prove. You, me, Nessa—we're all trying to show we belong here."

Finn felt a pang of recognition at Kieran's words. **He was**

right. They were all fighting their own battles, carrying their own insecurities. Finn's was his secret—his fear that he didn't belong here at all, that he wasn't really one of them.

Kieran glanced around, as if checking to make sure no one was listening, then leaned in slightly. "Look, I've been watching you."

Finn's heart skipped a beat. His hands clenched at his sides. **This is it. Kieran knows.**

"I don't know what it is," Kieran said, his eyes narrowing. "But something's different about you. You're not like the others."

Finn's chest tightened, his pulse quickening. **He knows.**

"I don't know what your deal is," Kieran continued, "but whatever it is, just… make sure it doesn't mess things up for the rest of us."

Before Finn could respond, Kieran turned and walked away, leaving Finn standing there, his heart racing. The cold air bit at his skin, but it was nothing compared to the icy dread spreading through his chest.

Kieran knew something was off. And if Kieran knew, it was only a matter of time before the others did too.

Chapter 8: The Team Fractures

The breaking point came during the **Christmas Tree Challenge**—a competition where each group had to design and decorate the most impressive tree in the courtyard. It was supposed to be a lighthearted, festive task, a chance for the recruits to show off their creativity and take a break from the more physically demanding challenges. But for Team Donner, it became something else entirely.

Master Evergreen gathered the recruits in the courtyard, his stern gaze sweeping over the teams as they stood beside their assigned trees. The sky was a pale, icy gray, the clouds heavy with the promise of snow, and the air had that biting crispness that seemed to seep into your bones no matter how many layers you wore. Despite the cold, the courtyard was a flurry of festive activity. Lights twinkled overhead, casting a warm glow over the snow-dusted ground, and the distant sound of carolers floated on the wind.

The Christmas trees stood tall and proud, each team given a blank canvas of green fir to transform into a masterpiece. Boxes of ornaments, garlands, tinsel, and twinkling lights had been provided, along with various materials for more creative decorations. It was supposed to be a celebration of holiday cheer—a way to tap into the magic of Christmas.

But for Team Donner, it was just another battlefield.

As the challenge began, the team scattered around the tree, grabbing decorations and tossing ideas into the mix. Elmer, ever the optimist, was the first to grab an ornament, his eyes lighting up as he pulled out a glittering gold star from the box. "This'll look great here!" he said, reaching up to place the star halfway up the tree.

"Why are you putting that ornament there?" Nessa snapped, her voice slicing through the chilly air like a blade. Her eyes narrowed as she stared at the star in Elmer's hand.

Elmer blinked, his usual cheer dimming just slightly as he shifted awkwardly. "Uh... because it looks nice?" he offered, his voice tinged with uncertainty.

"The star should go at the top," Nessa said, her tone hard as stone. "That's tradition, isn't it?"

Brigid, who had been silently hanging a string of twinkling lights, stepped forward, her voice calm but firm. "It's supposed to be about creativity, not just tradition," she reminded Nessa gently. "That's what Master Evergreen said."

Nessa shot Brigid a sharp look, her lips pressing into a thin line. "Creativity doesn't mean we ignore the basics," she said coolly. "Besides, a messy tree won't win us any points. We need to be smart about this."

Standing off to the side, Finn clenched his fists, his knuckles turning white. He had been biting his tongue all morning, trying to keep his frustration in check, but Nessa's constant need to control every decision was gnawing at him like a thorn under his skin. **Why couldn't she just let someone else take the lead for once?**

"Why don't you let someone else decide for a change?" Finn said, his voice low but firm, the words escaping before he could stop them.

Nessa's head whipped around, her eyes flaring with anger. "Excuse me?" Her voice was sharp, cutting through the air like a whip.

"I'm just saying," Finn continued, his heart pounding in his chest. "This isn't a one-elf show. You're always acting like your way is the only way, but we're supposed to be a team, aren't we?"

His words were sharper than he'd intended, but the frustration had been building for days, and he couldn't hold it back any longer.

Nessa's face flushed red, her eyes burning with fury. But there was something else in her expression too—something darker flickering just beneath the surface, like a secret being unearthed. "And what do you know about teamwork, Finn?" she spat. "You've been dragging us down since day one."

Finn's heart skipped a beat, her words hitting harder than he wanted to admit. His fists clenched at his sides. "Dragging you down?" he repeated, his voice rising with the swell of emotion. "I've been doing my best, just like everyone else. You're not the only one here who cares about this!"

Nessa's lips curled into a cold smile, her voice dropping to a chilling whisper. "Your best isn't good enough. You don't belong here, and everyone knows it. You're just pretending to keep up."

Finn's breath caught in his throat, the sting of her words hitting him like a slap. For a moment, the world around him seemed to blur. He could hear the distant murmur of the other teams, the soft jingling of bells from a nearby group hanging ornaments, but it all felt distant, drowned out by the sound of his own heartbeat thundering in his ears.

You don't belong here.

The words echoed in his mind, each repetition twisting the

knife deeper. She didn't know, did she? She couldn't. But the way she was looking at him, the anger and disdain in her eyes—it was as if she had seen right through him, seen the truth he had been desperately trying to hide.

"I—" Finn started, but the words stuck in his throat, lodged there by the fear rising in his chest. He didn't know how to respond. Nessa's accusation had cut too deep, too close to the truth he feared most.

Before he could say anything else, Master Evergreen's voice rang out through the courtyard, loud and clear. "Teams, gather for final judging!"

The argument was left hanging in the air, unresolved, as Team Donner fell into a tense silence. Finn could feel the weight of Nessa's words pressing down on him, squeezing the breath from his lungs. **You don't belong here.** It was the fear he had been trying to push down since the moment he set foot in Santa's School for Elves—the doubt that had been lurking in the back of his mind, growing stronger with each passing day.

Maybe Nessa was right. Maybe he didn't belong.

Chapter 9: The Breaking Point

Finn couldn't sleep that night.

Nessa's words circled in his mind, gnawing at him like a parasite: **You don't belong here.**

He tossed and turned in his bunk, his body restless with a tension he couldn't shake. Every creak of the wooden frame, every soft breath from his teammates only made his chest tighten more. Elmer's quiet snores above should have been a comfort, a reminder that he wasn't alone in this. But tonight, the sound seemed to underscore the distance between him and the others, a distance that felt as wide as a canyon.

What if she's right?

Finn squeezed his eyes shut, the question pressing in like a vice. No matter how tightly he closed his eyes, he couldn't block out the creeping fear. The moonlight filtered through the small dormitory window, casting faint shadows on the walls, but there was no peace in the stillness. The words kept replaying in his head: **What if I really don't belong here?**

He had been fighting this fear since the moment he arrived. Every day had been a battle to prove himself—not just to the others, but to himself. He'd worked harder than ever, pushing himself in every challenge, trying to show that he was more than just a leprechaun guarding a pot of gold. **But what if all his efforts were for nothing?** Nessa's words had struck too close to home. She didn't know his secret, not yet, but it felt like she had peered right through him, seen the lie he was living.

She could find out. The thought sent a chill down his spine. And if she did, what then? Would she tell the others? Would they turn on him before he had the chance to prove that he could be more than just a trickster leprechaun?

The weight of it all pressed down on him, and his thoughts began to spiral. **How long can I keep this up?**

Kieran's words echoed in his mind too: **"You're not like the**

others."

It had been subtle, a quiet observation, but Kieran's suspicions seemed to be growing with every passing day. Finn had been so careful, so meticulous about blending in, but no matter how hard he tried, it seemed like the elves around him could sense that something was off. Kieran, Nessa—they all seemed to see it, even if they didn't know what it was. It was there in Kieran's piercing gaze, in Nessa's constant criticism, in the way Finn faltered during tasks that seemed second nature to the others.

His heart pounded harder in his chest, each beat loud in the quiet dormitory. He had tried so hard to blend in, to be just another recruit, but the fear was gnawing at him, making it harder and harder to ignore the truth.

I don't belong here.

Finn clenched his fists under the blankets, trying to will himself to sleep. But it was no use. The truth was becoming impossible to ignore. He wasn't an elf. He wasn't supposed to be here at all. And the longer he stayed, the more fragile his façade became.

The alternative, though—**going back to Ireland**—was even worse. The thought of returning to his old life made his stomach churn. He couldn't go back to guarding a pot of gold, to pulling pranks and tricks just to pass the time. That life had become hollow, meaningless. He wanted more. **He wanted this.** But how long could he keep pretending?

With a heavy sigh, Finn sat up in his bunk, careful not to wake the others. The air in the room felt stifling, thick with his own unease. He needed to clear his head. Quietly, he grabbed his coat and slipped out of bed, moving like a shadow as he made his way toward the door.

The Courtyard

The courtyard was quiet when Finn stepped outside, the cold air hitting him like a slap to the face. Snow crunched softly beneath his boots as he walked, his breath fogging in the dim light from the lanterns that lined the pathways. The world seemed peaceful out here, untouched by the tension that gnawed at him inside. Above, the sky was clear, a blanket of stars twinkling against the deep blue of the night, each one like a distant spark of light in the vast expanse.

For a moment, the beauty of it all took his breath away.

This place—**the North Pole**—it was everything he had ever dreamed of. The snow-covered rooftops of the workshops, the warm glow of the lanterns casting gentle shadows on the cobblestone paths, the quiet magic that hummed through the air. It was a place of wonder, a place where dreams were made. And yet, here he was, feeling like the magic was slipping through his fingers, just out of reach.

Finn wandered aimlessly, his thoughts spinning in circles. Nessa's words echoed in his mind, sharp and unforgiving, but they weren't the only ones. Kieran's suspicion. Brigid's quiet concern. Every glance, every offhand comment seemed to pile on, weighing him down with the fear that they were all starting to figure him out.

He kicked at a patch of snow, watching it scatter across the path in front of him. **How long before they knew the truth?** How long before his secret unraveled?

"Are you alright, Finn?"

The voice startled him, pulling him out of his thoughts. He turned to see Brigid Cloverfield standing a few feet away, her quiet green eyes watching him with concern. She was wrapped in a thick cloak, her breath visible in the cold night air.

"I didn't mean to scare you," she said softly, stepping closer, her presence calm and steady. "I saw you come outside and thought I'd check on you."

Finn forced a smile, though it felt hollow. "Yeah. I'm fine. Just… couldn't sleep."

Brigid didn't say anything for a moment, just stood there watching him with that gentle, understanding gaze of hers. There was something comforting about her presence, something that made it hard for Finn to keep up the walls he'd built around himself.

"You don't have to pretend, you know," Brigid said quietly, her voice warm but firm. "We've all been feeling the pressure. This training—it's harder than I think any of us expected."

Finn let out a long breath, his shoulders sagging under the weight of his own thoughts. "Yeah… it's been tough."

Brigid's eyes softened, her calm gaze soothing some of the tension knotted in his chest. "Especially with Nessa breathing down your neck all the time."

Finn chuckled, the tension easing just a little. "She's something, huh?"

Brigid gave a small smile, her breath fogging in the cold air.

"She's difficult, but she means well. I think… I think she's just trying to prove herself, like the rest of us."

Finn nodded, though his mind was still buzzing with doubts. "Do you ever feel like…" He hesitated, the words sticking in his throat. He had been holding them in for so long, but now, in the quiet of the night, with Brigid's calm presence beside him, they threatened to spill out. "Do you ever feel like you don't belong here?"

Brigid tilted her head, considering his question for a moment. "Sometimes," she admitted softly. "It's easy to feel that way when you're surrounded by so many talented elves. Everyone's trying to prove themselves, and it can feel like… like maybe you're not good enough."

Finn's heart skipped a beat. **It was like she had plucked the thoughts straight out of his mind.**

"Exactly," he said quietly, his voice barely more than a whisper. "Like no matter how hard you try, you're always a step behind."

Brigid looked at him thoughtfully, her expression gentle and understanding. "I think we all feel that way sometimes. But you belong here, Finn. You've proven yourself more than once. Don't let anyone—including Nessa—make you think otherwise."

Finn swallowed hard, her words wrapping around him like a warm blanket. He wanted to believe her. He really did. But there was still that gnawing doubt, the secret that weighed on him like a lead weight in his chest. **If only she knew the truth.**

"I appreciate that, Brigid," Finn said, his voice quiet. "Really."

She smiled, and for a moment, the tension in Finn's chest eased just a little. "Come on, let's head back inside. It's freezing out here."

Finn nodded, following her back toward the dormitory, but his mind was still spinning with everything left unsaid. Brigid's words had helped, but they hadn't erased the truth. No matter what she said, no matter how much he wanted to believe her, the fact remained: **He didn't belong here.** And sooner or later, that truth would catch up to him.

Chapter 10: The Final Test

The next morning, the tension in Team Donner was palpable.

After the Christmas tree challenge and the heated argument with Nessa, things had reached a breaking point. The silence that stretched between them felt heavier than ever, like a weight none of them could shake off. Finn could feel it in the way they moved, the way they avoided each other's eyes as they prepared for the day's final challenge: **The Winter Obstacle Course**—a grueling test of physical endurance and teamwork that would push them all to their limits.

Master Evergreen stood at the front of the courtyard, his green coat billowing slightly in the crisp winter wind. His stern eyes scanned the recruits, as if measuring each of them for the challenge ahead. Behind him, the obstacle course stretched across the snowy field, a daunting maze of ice-covered walls, towering snowbanks, and narrow, treacherous paths. The air was sharp with the cold, the sky above a pale, steel gray.

Finn's stomach twisted as he stared at the course. He could already feel the weight of the day pressing down on him, a gnawing anxiety that had been with him since the moment he woke. He knew this was the most important challenge yet. **If they couldn't work together as a team, they would fail.** But after the argument with Nessa, the team already felt fractured, like a broken ornament held together by brittle glue.

Master Evergreen's voice cut through the stillness. "You will need to work together to complete the course," he said, his voice ringing out across the courtyard. "Only those who demonstrate true cooperation and determination will succeed."

Finn glanced at his teammates. Kieran stood at the edge of the group, his face expressionless, his dark eyes scanning the course as if already planning the best route. Elmer shifted nervously beside Finn, a small, worried frown on his usually cheerful face. Brigid stood quietly, her calm demeanor masking whatever tension might be bubbling beneath the surface. And Nessa... well, Nessa hadn't spoken to Finn since their argument. She stood rigid, arms crossed, her gaze fixed firmly ahead.

As Master Evergreen blew the whistle, the teams dashed toward the course, their breaths fogging in the cold air. Finn ran alongside Elmer, Brigid, and Kieran, his heart pounding in his chest as they reached the first obstacle—**an enormous wall of ice**, slick and treacherous, with only a few rough handholds carved into its frozen surface.

Merry
Christmas

Kieran, always quick and agile, was the first to scale the wall. His movements were smooth, effortless, as if he'd done this a hundred times before. In seconds, he was at the top, turning to help Brigid, who followed closely behind with careful, deliberate steps. Elmer struggled a bit more—his hands slipping on the icy surface—but he eventually made it with Kieran's help, his face flushed with the effort.

Finn stood at the base of the wall, his heart hammering in his chest. The icy wall loomed above him, cold and unforgiving. **He wasn't as nimble as the others**, and the slick surface looked treacherous, each handhold more slippery than the last. The memory of his failures in previous challenges crept into his mind, clawing at his confidence.

"Come on, Finn!" Elmer called from above, his voice full of encouragement, though his breath came in sharp puffs of cold air. "You've got this!"

Finn gritted his teeth, gripping the nearest handhold. His fingers were already numb from the cold, and as he began to climb, the ice bit into his hands like tiny daggers. **Just keep moving**, he told himself. **One handhold at a time.**

But halfway up the wall, his foot slipped. His grip faltered. And before he could react, he lost his balance completely, tumbling backward. He hit the ground hard, the wind knocked from his lungs as he landed in the snow.

"Finn!" Brigid's voice was full of concern, but it only made the sting of failure worse.

Finn's heart sank. The others were already at the top, waiting for him, and he had just slowed them down. Again. **The**

weight of his failure settled heavily on his shoulders, pressing down with a familiar ache. His breath came in short gasps as he scrambled to his feet, brushing the snow off his coat, his cheeks burning with embarrassment.

Before he could attempt the climb again, Kieran's voice called down from above. "Finn, grab the rope."

Finn looked up to see Kieran lowering a rope down the side of the wall, his expression unreadable. For a moment, Finn hesitated. **Pride warred with his need for help.** He didn't want to rely on the others. He didn't want to seem weak, not after everything.

But there was no time to waste. **The course wouldn't wait for him to swallow his pride.** Gritting his teeth, Finn grabbed the rope, feeling the burn of cold against his palms. With Kieran's steady pull and Elmer's encouragement, he finally made it to the top. His breath came in ragged, heavy bursts as he collapsed in the snow, exhaustion already tugging at his limbs.

"Thanks," Finn muttered, the weight of his embarrassment settling over him like a lead blanket.

Kieran gave a curt nod, his expression still unreadable. "Let's keep moving."

The Narrow Path

The next part of the obstacle course was **a narrow, winding path**, barely wide enough for one person, with sheer, snow-covered embankments on either side. The ground was slick with ice, each step more treacherous than the last. One wrong move, and they'd slide down the embankment, losing precious time.

Brigid took the lead, her movements careful and precise. Her feet made almost no sound as she navigated the path, her balance steady. Finn followed close behind, every muscle in his body tense as he focused on keeping his footing. His breath was shallow, each step feeling like it could be his last. He could hear Kieran and Elmer behind him, their footsteps muffled by the snow, but his focus was on the path in front of him—on making it to the end without slipping.

But halfway through the path, a sharp shout rang out from behind.

"Watch out!"

Finn whipped his head around just in time to see Elmer's feet fly out from under him. In an instant, Elmer was tumbling down the embankment, sliding on the ice before landing in a heap at the bottom.

Without thinking, Finn scrambled down after him. His feet slipped on the icy slope, sending him skidding down the embankment, but he didn't care. He reached Elmer's side, his heart pounding in his chest. "Are you alright?"

Elmer groaned, wincing as he sat up, snow clinging to his coat. "I think so... Just bruised my pride."

Finn let out a breath of relief, pulling Elmer to his feet. But when he glanced back up at the path, his stomach sank. They had fallen behind. Brigid and Kieran were already near the end, waiting for them, but the other teams were pulling ahead. **Time was slipping away, and failure loomed over**

them like a shadow.

"We have to move," Finn said, urgency tightening his voice. "Come on."

With Elmer at his side, they made their way back up the embankment, slipping and sliding on the ice, their breath coming in ragged gasps. **Every step felt like a battle.**

The Final Obstacle

The final obstacle loomed ahead: **a towering chimney**, wide enough for a single person to climb through, but smooth as glass. There were no handholds, no ledges—just smooth walls that seemed to stretch endlessly upward. **The only way up was by working together.**

"We'll need to boost each other up," Kieran said, his tone brisk and efficient. His eyes flickered toward Finn. "You go first."

Finn hesitated. **After all his failures, the thought of going first felt like a daunting task.** What if he messed up again? What if he let the team down in the final stretch? But there was no time to argue, and he couldn't afford to let his fear control him now. He nodded, stepping forward.

Brigid and Kieran crouched down, cupping their hands to give Finn a boost. With their help, he hoisted himself up into the narrow chimney, his legs scrambling for purchase on the smooth walls. **The space pressed in around him, tight and confining,** and his arms ached as he pulled himself up, inch by inch. The smooth stone seemed to resist every effort, and his muscles screamed with the effort.

But he couldn't let the team down. Not now. **Not when they**

had come this far.

After what felt like an eternity, Finn finally reached the top, pulling himself onto solid ground. His chest heaved with the effort, his hands trembling with exhaustion. But there was no time to rest. He turned back, extending his hand to Elmer, who was next to climb.

One by one, they made it to the top, their faces flushed with exertion, their breaths coming in short, sharp gasps. **Every muscle ached**, but they were close—so close to the finish.

As they reached the final stretch of the course, the other teams were just finishing. The air was filled with cheers and shouts of triumph as the last recruits crossed the finish line.

Finn's heart sank. **They hadn't won.** They hadn't been fast enough.

But as he looked around at his team, he saw something that surprised him. Despite their exhaustion, despite the setbacks and the tension that had hung over them all day, there was a quiet sense of pride in their eyes. They had made it through the course together. They hadn't given up.

For the first time, Finn realized that maybe it wasn't about winning. Maybe it was about something more—**teamwork, resilience, trust**. Those were the things that mattered. And in that moment, despite everything, Finn felt a small flicker of hope.

Maybe, just maybe, he did belong here after all.

Chapter 11: The Secret Unveiled

Later that evening, the recruits gathered in the great hall, their breath still visible in the cold air from the courtyard. The hall was a grand and imposing space, its high ceilings adorned with twinkling lights and evergreen garlands. The warmth from the great hearth at the far end of the room did little to ease the nervous energy that buzzed through the crowd of recruits. Finn could feel it too—his heart still heavy from the day's events, though the lingering sense of camaraderie with his team helped to soften the weight.

The recruits had come far. They were tired, bruised, but determined. As Finn stood among his teammates, the flickering light from the hearth casting long shadows across the room, he couldn't shake the tension that curled in his chest. The obstacle course was over, but what came next would decide their future.

At the front of the hall, Master Evergreen stood tall, his expression as stern and unreadable as ever, though Finn noticed a faint gleam of approval in his eyes. He scanned the room, his gaze resting on each team in turn, his presence commanding silence. The only sound was the crackling of the fire as everyone waited with bated breath for him to speak.

"You have all completed the Winter Obstacle Course," Master Evergreen said, his deep voice carrying through the hall like a steady drumbeat. "Some of you finished quickly, others struggled, but every one of you showed resilience and determination."

Finn's heart pounded in his chest. His mind replayed every

misstep, every stumble. They hadn't been the fastest. They hadn't been the most coordinated. He could still feel the sting of his earlier failures, the way his grip had slipped on the ice, the way they'd fallen behind. **How could they possibly stand out among the other teams?**

But as Finn glanced around at his teammates—at Elmer, whose endless optimism never faltered, at Brigid, whose quiet strength had kept them steady, and even at Kieran, who stood with his arms crossed but a look of determination in his eyes— he felt a flicker of pride. **They had made it through together.** And that had to count for something.

Master Evergreen's voice continued, clear and unwavering. "But as you all know, it is not only speed that determines success. It is your ability to work together, to overcome obstacles as a team, that truly matters."

Work together. The words sank in, and Finn felt the knot in his stomach twist. **Had they really worked together?** He thought of the tension with Nessa, the way they had struggled to find common ground, the way they had faltered during the challenge. And yet... they had made it. Somehow, they had crossed the finish line as one.

The hall was silent, the air thick with anticipation as Master Evergreen began to announce the results. Finn's heart raced. They hadn't won—he was sure of that. But maybe, just maybe, their teamwork had been enough to earn them some kind of recognition.

"And now," Master Evergreen said, his eyes scanning the crowd, "for the team that demonstrated the most resilience and teamwork in the face of adversity... Team Donner."

Finn blinked. **What?**

Shock rippled through him, freezing him in place. Had he heard that right? **Team Donner?**

The hall erupted into applause, the sound filling the air like a wave crashing over him. Finn stood frozen, his mind struggling to catch up. **They had won?** Despite everything, despite the arguments, the falls, the slips—they had won recognition for their efforts.

Beside him, Elmer let out a whoop of excitement, clapping Finn on the back with enough force to nearly knock him over. "We did it!" Elmer beamed, his face flushed with pride. Even Kieran, usually so reserved, allowed himself a small, satisfied smile.

Finn's chest swelled with emotion. The applause felt like a warm blanket wrapping around him, and for the first time in a long while, he allowed himself to bask in the moment. They had done it. Despite all the setbacks, despite the lingering tension in the team, **they had proven themselves.**

As they stood there, their teammates exchanging looks of pride and disbelief, Finn felt a sense of belonging that he hadn't felt in weeks. Maybe, just maybe, he could fit in here. Maybe this was proof that he didn't have to be perfect, that he didn't have to hide behind his insecurities. **They had done it together, and that was what mattered.**

But just as the applause began to fade, Finn's heart skipped a beat.

Out of the corner of his eye, he saw a figure moving through the crowd—Master Alder, one of the older, more respected mentors at the school. His steps were deliberate, his sharp eyes locked intently on Finn, and there was something in his gaze that sent a chill down Finn's spine.

Finn's breath caught in his throat. **This is it.** His chest tightened, panic rising like a wave. He knew, without a doubt, that this was the moment he had been dreading. **His secret was about to be exposed.**

Master Alder approached slowly, the applause and cheers fading into background noise as Finn's world narrowed to that one figure. Each step the older elf took seemed to echo in Finn's ears, like a countdown to disaster. His palms grew damp, his heart pounding so hard it felt like it might burst from his chest.

When Master Alder finally reached him, Finn could barely breathe. The mentor's sharp eyes seemed to pierce right through him, and the weight of that gaze was suffocating. **He knows.** Finn could feel it in his bones. **He knows I'm not an elf.**

"Finn O'Malley," Master Alder said, his voice quiet but firm, cutting through the haze of Finn's fear like a knife. "May I speak with you?"

The room seemed to spin for a moment. Finn's mouth went dry, and his stomach churned with dread. Every muscle in his body screamed for him to run, to escape, but his legs felt like lead, rooted to the spot.

He managed a nod, though his voice failed him. He could feel the eyes of his teammates on him, could sense their confusion. **What's going on?** they must have been thinking. But Finn couldn't meet their gazes. He couldn't bear to see the look of betrayal that might cross their faces when the truth came out.

Master Alder gestured for Finn to follow, and with shaking legs, Finn obeyed. His mind raced with panic, every worst-case scenario flashing through his head in vivid detail. **Would he be expelled? Would they drag him out of the North Pole and send him back to Ireland?** He couldn't go back. Not after everything. Not after he had tasted what it felt like to be part of something more.

As they left the great hall, the noise of the celebration dimmed behind them. Finn's breath came in shallow, ragged gasps as they stepped into a quiet corridor, the flickering light from the lanterns casting long, eerie shadows on the stone walls.

Master Alder stopped, turning to face Finn. His eyes were still sharp, but there was something else in his expression now—something Finn couldn't quite place. Was it... curiosity?

"Do you know why I've brought you here, Finn?" Master Alder asked, his voice calm but tinged with something Finn couldn't read.

Finn swallowed hard, his throat tight. **This is it.** He opened his mouth to speak, but the words stuck, his fear choking him.

Master Alder watched him for a moment, then took a step closer. "There's something different about you, Finn," he said, his tone softer now, though still edged with that same sharpness. "I've been watching you since you arrived. You've worked hard, you've shown determination... but there's something you're hiding, isn't there?"

Finn's heart pounded in his ears. The walls felt like they were closing in on him. **Should he tell the truth? Should he admit everything right here, right now?**

"I... I..." Finn stammered, his voice barely more than a whisper. **Tell him.** The words screamed in his mind, but he couldn't force them out. **What would happen when the truth finally came to light?**

Master Alder waited, his gaze steady, unyielding.

And Finn knew, in that moment, that the secret he had been so desperately clinging to was about to unravel.

Chapter 12: The Secret Comes Out

Finn's heart pounded in his chest as he followed Master Alder through the dimly lit corridors of the school. The sound of applause from the great hall still echoed faintly in his ears, but it felt distant now—like something from a dream, slipping away into the fog of reality. All that mattered was what was about to happen.

Master Alder walked with a quiet authority, his tall, wiry frame casting long shadows in the flickering lamplight. His silver hair gleamed in the dimness, and his sharp eyes—eyes that seemed to see through everything—remained fixed ahead. The silence between them was suffocating. Finn's palms were damp with sweat, his breath shallow and uneven. He hadn't exchanged more than a few polite words with Alder before tonight, but he knew the elf by reputation. **Alder wasn't just any mentor.** He was one of Santa's most trusted advisors—known for his fairness, yes, but also for his unwavering commitment to the rules.

Finn's stomach twisted with dread. **If Alder knew his secret, this could be the end.**

The corridors seemed to stretch endlessly, the weight of each step growing heavier as Finn's mind raced. **Would they send him home? Would they expel him in disgrace?** He had worked so hard to be here, to prove that he could belong, but now... **now it felt like everything was slipping through his fingers.**

Alder led Finn to a small, private study tucked away in a quiet corner of the school. It was a cozy, unassuming room, its walls lined with shelves overflowing with old, weathered books. A single lantern cast a warm glow across the space, but the shadows it created seemed to dance ominously along the walls. The flickering light only deepened the tension gnawing at Finn's insides.

Alder stepped inside, closing the door behind them with a soft, deliberate click that seemed to echo far too loudly in the small space. Finn's legs felt weak, and he hovered near the door, unwilling to move any further into the room. **It felt like stepping into a cage.**

"Please," Alder said, his voice calm but firm, gesturing to a small wooden table in the center of the room. "Take a seat."

Finn hesitated, his pulse racing. His feet felt like they were stuck in the snow, but finally, he forced himself to move. He sat down at the table, his fingers gripping the edge of the chair so tightly his knuckles turned white. His mind was spinning

with excuses, explanations, ways to talk his way out of this—
but none of them felt strong enough to hold up under Master
Alder's piercing gaze.

Alder sat down across from him, folding his hands on the
table, his sharp eyes studying Finn with an intensity that made
it hard to breathe. For a long, agonizing moment, there was
nothing but silence. Finn could hear the faint crackle of the
lantern's flame, the rustle of fabric as Alder adjusted his seat—
but mostly, he could hear the pounding of his own heartbeat,
loud and frantic in his ears.

Finally, after what felt like an eternity, Master Alder spoke.

"Finn," he began, his voice low but steady, "I've been watching
you for some time now. You've shown remarkable skill, especially given the challenges you've faced. Your determination is
impressive."

Finn blinked, his heart skipping a beat. Was that... a compli-
ment? He hadn't expected that. **Was Alder trying to soften
the blow?**

"But," Alder continued, and Finn's stomach lurched at the
word, "there's something... different about you. Something I
can't quite put my finger on."

Finn's breath hitched. His throat felt dry, and his hands trembled slightly as they rested in his lap. **He knows.** The thought
was a weight pressing down on his chest. **He knows.**

Alder leaned back slightly, his gaze never wavering. "You're not
like the others, are you?"

The question hung in the air, heavy and damning. Finn's chest tightened with fear, a knot forming in his stomach. This was it. **The moment he had been dreading since the day he arrived.** Alder didn't just suspect—he knew something was off. Maybe he hadn't figured it out entirely yet, but Finn could feel the walls closing in.

"I—I don't know what you mean," Finn stammered, though even as the words left his mouth, he knew they were useless. There was no hiding it anymore. **The truth was clawing its way to the surface, whether he wanted it to or not.**

Alder's eyes softened, just a fraction. "Finn, I'm not here to accuse you of anything. But I need you to be honest with me. You're hiding something, and whatever it is, it's important that we address it."

The calm in Alder's voice should have been reassuring, but it wasn't. If anything, it made the moment more terrifying. Finn could feel the weight of the secret he had been carrying pressing down on him, the guilt, the fear, the constant anxiety that had been gnawing at him since day one. **He couldn't do it anymore.** He couldn't keep up the lie.

His pulse raced, his heart thundering in his chest like a drum. His mind screamed at him to lie again, to make something up, to deny it all—but another part of him, the part that had been burdened by this secret for so long, was desperate to finally let it all out.

He took a deep breath, his hands trembling in his lap. "I... I'm not an elf," he said quietly, his voice barely above a whisper.

Master Alder didn't react immediately. He simply watched Finn, his expression calm but unreadable. "Go on."

Finn hesitated, his heart hammering in his chest. **This was it.** The truth. He could feel it bubbling up, ready to spill out, no matter how hard he had tried to suppress it.

"I'm... I'm a leprechaun," Finn blurted, the words rushing out in a breathless confession. "I wasn't born here. I don't have the same talents as the other recruits. I lied on my application because—because I wanted to be part of this world. I wanted to do something more than just guard gold and play tricks. I thought... I thought maybe I could belong here."

The silence that followed his confession was deafening. Finn could barely breathe. He felt like the weight of the entire room was pressing down on him, crushing him. **He had done it.** He had finally told the truth. But now, in the echoing quiet, it felt like the world was waiting to collapse in on him.

Master Alder didn't speak right away. He sat back in his chair, his eyes thoughtful as he absorbed Finn's words. His expression remained unreadable, and the longer the silence stretched on, the more Finn's nerves frayed.

"A leprechaun," Alder said softly, as if testing the word on his tongue. "I can't say I've ever encountered one in our ranks before."

Finn's chest tightened. "I know it's against the rules," he said quickly, his voice trembling with fear. "I know I wasn't supposed to apply. But I just... I couldn't go back to the life I had. I wanted something more."

Alder nodded slowly, his eyes still fixed on Finn. "You've broken the rules," he said, his tone serious but not harsh. "But you've also shown dedication, resilience, and a desire to be part of something bigger than yourself."

Finn blinked, his heart pounding. **Was that... approval?** He hadn't expected this. He had prepared himself for anger, for rejection, for the worst possible outcome. But Alder wasn't reacting the way he had feared.

"I'm not going to make any decisions tonight," Alder said, standing up slowly, his gaze still locked on Finn. "This is a matter that needs to be discussed with the headmaster and the council."

Finn's stomach twisted with dread. "So... what happens now?"

Alder's eyes softened again, just slightly. "You've proven yourself, Finn. That will be taken into consideration. But rules are rules, and we will need to decide how to proceed. For now, return to your dormitory. I'll speak with you again tomorrow."

Finn nodded, though the dread in his stomach remained. "Thank you," he said quietly, though the words felt hollow in his mouth. He wasn't sure what he was thanking Alder for—his fairness, perhaps, or the fact that he hadn't been kicked out on the spot.

As Finn left the study and made his way back through the winding corridors, his mind was a whirlwind of emotions. Fear, relief, uncertainty—each one crashing into him in waves. **He had finally told the truth.** The weight of his secret was gone, but in its place was a new, heavier burden. **What would happen next?**

He didn't know. And that uncertainty, that lingering sense of the unknown, gnawed at him with every step he took.

Chapter 13: Facing the Truth

The next morning, the tension in Dormitory 17 was thicker than ever.

Finn hadn't told anyone about his conversation with Master Alder, but the weight of his secret hung over him like a storm cloud, dark and unyielding. He could feel it pressing down on him with every step he took, in the hushed voices of his teammates, in the curious glances thrown his way. **It was only a matter of time before the truth came crashing down.**

Elmer, always perceptive, had noticed something was off. "You alright, Finn?" he asked quietly that morning, his brow furrowed with concern. They were seated on their bunks, the dormitory buzzing with the usual early-morning activity, but Finn hadn't said more than a few words all day.

Finn forced a smile, though his stomach churned with anxiety. "I'm fine," he lied, his voice a little too flat. "Just... a lot on my mind."

Elmer gave him a long, searching look, his bright eyes narrowing slightly. "You've been acting weird since last night. You sure everything's okay?"

There was something so genuine in Elmer's concern that Finn's heart twisted with guilt. **Elmer didn't know.** None of them knew. And the longer Finn kept this secret, the more it felt like a betrayal. He swallowed hard, wishing he could just confide in his friend—but the thought of what might happen if Elmer knew the truth made Finn's throat tighten.

"Yeah," Finn said quickly, the words feeling hollow. "I'm good.

Just tired."

Elmer watched him for another moment, his frown deepening, but he didn't press further. "Alright," he said finally, his voice softening. "But if you need to talk..."

"Thanks, Elmer," Finn interrupted, his voice tight. He couldn't let Elmer's kindness break through his walls—not now. Not yet.

By midday, the rumors had started to spread. **Word had gotten out** that Master Alder had called a meeting with the headmaster and the council. Finn's heart raced every time he overheard a whisper, every time he caught snippets of conversations from passing recruits.

"What do you think it's about?"

"I heard someone broke the rules."

"Maybe someone's getting sent home..."

Each word sent a fresh wave of panic crashing through Finn's mind. **Was this about him?** Was the council meeting right now, deciding his fate? **Would they call him in today?** Would they give him a chance to explain himself—or would they simply decide to send him home, without a second thought?

The anxiety gnawed at him all day, a relentless force that made it impossible to focus. He moved through his lessons in a fog, barely registering what was being said or what tasks were being assigned. His mind was too consumed with the knowledge that, at any moment, the truth could come crashing down.

By the time evening rolled around, Finn felt like he was on the verge of breaking. He couldn't keep this up. He couldn't keep pretending everything was fine when the truth was hanging over him like a sword, ready to fall at any moment. **He had never felt so alone.**

And then, just as Finn was about to retreat to the dormitory for the night, he heard the voice he had been dreading.

"Finn."

The single word cut through the cold air like a blade, stopping him in his tracks. His heart plummeted into his stomach as he turned and saw **Kieran Shadowbrook** standing a few feet away, his arms crossed tightly over his chest. The look on Kieran's face was hard, his dark eyes narrowed with suspicion. There was no warmth in his voice, no trace of the camaraderie they had once shared—only cold accusation.

Finn's stomach dropped. **Kieran had always been watching him.** He had always sensed something was off, always questioned Finn's place here. And now... now it looked like Kieran was ready to confront him about what he had suspected all along.

"We need to talk," Kieran said, his tone leaving no room for argument.

Finn's throat tightened, a wave of fear washing over him. "About what?"

"Don't play dumb, Finn," Kieran snapped, his voice sharp as ice. He took a step closer, his eyes narrowing dangerously. "I've been watching you. You've been acting strange since you got here, and I want to know why."

The force of Kieran's words hit Finn like a punch to the gut. **He knows.** Finn's mind raced, desperately searching for a way out, but there was none. Kieran had him cornered, and Finn could feel the walls closing in, the truth clawing its way up his throat.

"I... I don't know what you're talking about," Finn said weakly, though even as the words left his mouth, he knew it was useless. **The lie felt heavy and brittle, ready to shatter.**

Kieran's eyes flashed with anger, his jaw tightening. "Cut the act!" he spat, stepping forward, his voice low and dangerous. "You're hiding something, and I know it. You've been lying to us."

The accusation hit Finn hard. His heart raced, panic flaring in his chest. His hands trembled at his sides, his pulse pounding in his ears. **This was it.** He could feel it slipping away from him, the secret he had held so tightly for so long.

"I don't belong here," Finn blurted out, the words spilling from him in a rush, his voice cracking under the weight of the confession. "I'm not... I'm not an elf."

Kieran's expression didn't change immediately, but there was a flicker of something in his dark eyes—surprise, confusion, disbelief. "What are you talking about?" he demanded, his voice a harsh whisper.

Finn took a deep breath, his heart hammering in his chest. **It was all over now.** He couldn't lie anymore, couldn't pretend. "I'm not an elf," he repeated, his voice quieter, weaker. "I'm a leprechaun. I lied on my application. I shouldn't be here."

For a moment, Kieran just stared at him, his eyes searching Finn's face as if trying to make sense of the confession. The silence between them felt like it stretched on for an eternity, every second thick with tension. Then, slowly, Kieran's expression hardened.

"A leprechaun," he said, his voice dripping with disbelief, the word almost a sneer. "You're a leprechaun?"

Finn nodded, his heart sinking deeper with every breath. "I didn't mean to lie," he said quickly, his voice shaking. "I just... I wanted to be part of this. I wanted to prove that I could do more than just guard gold and play tricks."

Kieran's face twisted with anger, his eyes flashing with betrayal. "So you lied to all of us," he said, his voice cold and sharp. "You've been pretending this whole time, letting us think you were one of us. Do you even care about the team? About everything we've been through?"

Finn's chest tightened with guilt. "Of course I care!" he said, his voice rising with desperation. "I've worked hard. I've been trying to prove myself. I didn't want to deceive anyone—I just... I didn't have a choice."

Kieran's jaw clenched, his fists tightening at his sides. "You always had a choice, Finn," he said, his voice low and biting. "You just chose to lie."

The words hit Finn like a blow, knocking the air from his lungs. He stood there, frozen in place, as Kieran shook his head, his expression hardening further.

With that, Kieran turned on his heel and walked away, his footsteps crunching in the snow as he disappeared into the night, leaving Finn standing there—alone in the cold.

Chapter 14: The Council's Decision

The next morning, Finn was summoned to the council chamber.

The moment he had feared—the moment that had haunted his every thought—was finally here.

His heart thundered in his chest as he made his way through the grand, snow-dusted hallways of the school. The cold air bit at his cheeks, but it did little to numb the growing sense of dread that coiled in his stomach. Each step felt heavier than the last, and the towering stone walls seemed to close in around him as if they were pushing him toward his inevitable fate. **What would happen when he stood before the council?**

When Finn reached the entrance to the council chamber, the large wooden doors loomed before him, cracked open just enough to let a sliver of light spill out into the hall. It felt like the line between two worlds—the one he was leaving behind, and the uncertain one waiting just beyond.

Master Alder stood at the entrance, his silver hair gleaming in the soft light, his expression serious but not unkind. "Come in, Finn," he said quietly, stepping aside to allow Finn to enter.

With a deep, shaky breath, Finn stepped through the door.

Inside, the chamber was large and imposing, its stone walls lined with ancient banners and tapestries that whispered of centuries of tradition. A large wooden table dominated the center of the room, around which sat the council members—figures Finn had seen only from a distance, each of them representing the highest authority at the school. Their faces were solemn, their eyes watchful. **They were here to decide his fate.**

At the head of the table sat **Headmaster Hollyberry**, an ancient elf with a long silver beard that brushed the table in front of him. His eyes, though wise and kind, were grave as they met Finn's. To his right was **Master Evergreen**, his sharp gaze fixed on Finn with the same intensity he always carried. The others—elders of the council—watched in silence, their expressions unreadable.

Finn's stomach twisted with nerves. **This was it.** The moment that would decide everything. His future hung in the balance, and all he could do was stand there, his hands trembling at his sides as the weight of the moment pressed down on him like a crushing force.

Headmaster Hollyberry spoke first, his voice deep and resonant. "Finn O'Malley," he began, each word deliberate, "we have been made aware of your... situation. Master Alder has informed us of your confession, and we have deliberated on how to proceed."

Finn swallowed hard, his heart racing in his chest. He could feel the panic bubbling up inside him, threatening to overwhelm him. **This was it.** He had confessed, but would it be enough to save him?

"You have broken the rules," the headmaster continued, his

eyes soft but stern. "Santa's School for Elves was founded on principles of honesty, trust, and integrity. By lying on your application, you violated those principles."

The words hit Finn like a hammer, his chest tightening with dread. **He knew this was coming.** He had known the moment he submitted that false application that he was breaking the rules. And yet, hearing it spoken aloud, in this room filled with the most powerful elves in the North Pole, felt like a blow to the gut.

Headmaster Hollyberry's gaze never wavered as he continued. "Such actions cannot be taken lightly, and there are consequences for deceiving those around you."

Finn's breath caught in his throat. **This is it.** He braced himself, his mind already racing ahead to the worst case scenario. **Would they send him home?** Would they expel him from the North Pole, banish him from this world he had fought so hard to be part of? The idea of returning to his old life—guarding gold and pulling pranks—felt like a nightmare. **He couldn't go back.**

"But," the headmaster said, and Finn blinked, startled by the shift in his tone. **But?**

Hollyberry's expression softened, just a fraction. "We have also taken into account your actions during your time here. You have shown great courage, determination, and a willingness to learn. You have demonstrated qualities that we value in all of our students, regardless of where they come from."

Finn's heart skipped a beat. **Was he hearing this right?** He had prepared himself for rejection, for dismissal, but there was something in the headmaster's eyes—something warmer, more understanding than Finn had expected.

Headmaster Hollyberry leaned forward slightly, his wise eyes locking onto Finn's. "It is clear to us that you are not just a leprechaun pretending to be an elf. You have proven that you have the heart of an elf. And for that, we are willing to offer you a second chance."

Finn's breath caught in his throat. **A second chance?**

For a moment, the world seemed to blur around him. He could hardly believe what he was hearing. **A second chance?** He hadn't been expelled? He hadn't been sent home? Relief surged through him, so powerful it nearly took his breath away. **He wasn't being cast out.**

Headmaster Hollyberry smiled gently, a warmth in his eyes that made Finn's chest swell with gratitude. "You will be allowed to remain at Santa's School for Elves," the headmaster continued, his voice calm and reassuring. "However, this second chance comes with conditions. You will be expected to follow all the rules, and you will be held to the same standards as every other student."

Finn felt a wave of emotion wash over him, his hands trembling with the force of it. He had been given another chance—**a chance to stay, to prove himself.** He had come so close to losing it all, and yet... they had given him their trust. They had seen something in him worth keeping.

"Thank you," Finn said quickly, his voice trembling with emotion. His heart was pounding so hard in his chest he thought it might burst. "I promise... I won't let you down."

Headmaster Hollyberry's smile widened, the kindness in his eyes brightening. "We believe in second chances, Finn. Don't waste yours."

Finn nodded, his throat tight with emotion. **He wouldn't waste it.** He would do everything he could to prove he belonged here—not just as a leprechaun, but as a student worthy of the North Pole. He had been given a gift, and he would fight with everything he had to honor it.

As he left the council chamber, the weight that had been pressing down on him for so long finally began to lift. The air felt lighter, the hallway wider, and for the first time in what felt like days, Finn could breathe again.

The stone walls that had seemed so cold and imposing now felt warm, inviting. The snow-dusted hallways stretched out before him, no longer filled with dread but with possibility. **This was his second chance.** And he wouldn't take it for granted.

Chapter 15: The Aftermath

By lunchtime, the entire school knew.

Finn O'Malley wasn't an elf. He was a leprechaun.

The news spread like wildfire, whispered from one recruit to the next until it seemed like the walls themselves were buzzing with gossip. Wherever Finn went, the whispers followed—soft murmurs just loud enough for him to catch fragments, little bites of disbelief and curiosity that felt like tiny barbs sinking into his skin.

"A leprechaun? Can you believe it?"

"Why would he lie like that?"

"I always knew something was off..."

The stares were even worse. Finn could feel them on him, sharp as daggers, every time he entered a room. Even when people pretended to look away, he could still sense their eyes trailing after him, lingering just long enough to make his skin crawl. He walked through the hallways with his head down, hands shoved deep into his pockets, trying to ignore the knots of tension that had taken root in his stomach.

It was exactly what he had feared. No matter how much he had wanted to belong here, to be accepted, his lie had shattered the fragile trust he had built. And now he had to face the consequences.

But not everyone was against him.

Elmer had been the first to find him after the news broke, his round face full of concern and loyalty. "We don't care if you're a leprechaun," Elmer had said, his voice firm with conviction. His hand landed on Finn's shoulder with a reassuring clap, as if that one gesture could chase away all the doubts and whispers swirling around them. "You're still Finn, and you're still part of our team."

Finn had blinked at him, surprised by the simple kindness. "Thanks, Elmer," he had muttered, feeling a mix of gratitude and guilt rising in his chest. He didn't deserve Elmer's loyalty— not after deceiving everyone.

Brigid had been just as supportive, her quiet presence a balm to Finn's frayed nerves. "Everyone makes mistakes," she had said gently, her soft green eyes meeting his with understanding. "What matters is what you do next." She hadn't pressed him for details, hadn't asked for explanations—just stood by him with a calm, unshakeable acceptance that made Finn's chest tighten with emotion.

Even Seamus, the mischievous elf who was always quick with a joke, had offered a supportive grin. "Hey, at least now we know who to blame for all the gold disappearing," he had quipped, giving Finn a wink. The joke had been lighthearted, but there was no malice in it—only an attempt to ease the tension. Finn had managed a small smile, grateful for the effort.

But not everyone was as forgiving.

Nessa Goldenbloom had been the loudest voice of disbelief when she found out. Her eyes had gone wide, her lips curling into a sneer as she stared at Finn, the disdain practically radiating off of her.

"A leprechaun?" she had scoffed, her voice loud enough for half the room to hear. "I knew something was off about you. You're not like the rest of us. You never were."

Finn had wanted to say something in response, to defend himself, but the words caught in his throat. Nessa's sharp gaze had cut into him, and all he could do was stand there and take it, the weight of her judgment pressing down on him like a stone.

And then, of course, there was **Kieran**.

After their confrontation the night before, Kieran hadn't spoken a word to Finn. He had kept his distance, his expression cold and distant whenever their paths crossed. There was no more sharp suspicion in his gaze—just quiet, simmering anger. **The betrayal was still raw**, and Finn could feel the weight of it every time Kieran's eyes flicked toward him. There was no mistaking it: for Kieran, the damage had been done.

Finn couldn't blame him. He had lied to all of them. He had deceived the team, his friends—people who had trusted him. And now he had to face the fact that not everyone would forgive him so easily. Some people, like Nessa and Kieran, might never forgive him.

The day dragged on, each hour passing like a slow grind of anxiety and guilt. Finn moved through the motions of his tasks, but his mind was far from focused. Every whisper, every sideways glance, felt like a reminder of how much he had lost.

But as the afternoon faded into evening, and the long shadows stretched across the snowy courtyards, Finn began to realize something important.

Yes, he had made mistakes. **Yes, he had lied.** He had broken the trust of the people around him, and the weight of that would stay with him for a long time. But there was something else, something deeper stirring in his chest.

He had also worked harder than he ever had in his life.

From the moment he had set foot in Santa's School for Elves, Finn had been determined to prove himself. He had faced challenges that had pushed him to his limits—challenges that would have been difficult for anyone, let alone someone pretending to be something they weren't. He had stumbled, yes, but he had also gotten back up. He had fought for his place here. And now, despite everything, despite the whispers and the stares, **he had been given a second chance.**

A second chance to do things right.

As Finn lay in bed that night, staring up at the ceiling of the dormitory, he let the events of the day swirl around him. The uncertainty, the fear, the guilt—it was all still there, sitting heavy in his chest. But beneath it, something new had begun to take root.

Resolve.

He wasn't going to waste this second chance. He wasn't going to let the whispers or the stares define him. He had a lot to prove—to the council, to his team, to the school—but most importantly, to himself.

Finn took a deep breath, the cool night air filling his lungs, and for the first time in what felt like weeks, he felt a flicker of hope. He had a long way to go, but he wasn't giving up. **He wouldn't give up.**

He was Finn O'Malley, and he was going to make the most of his second chance.

Chapter 16: Rebuilding Trust

The days following Finn's confession were a strange mix of relief and tension.

On one hand, the weight of his secret had finally been lifted. There were no more lies, no more pretending. He could breathe again without the fear of being discovered lurking in

the back of his mind. But the relief was fleeting, overshad-
owed by the cold reality of how others saw him now. **Everything had changed.**

The reactions from his peers were mixed at best.

There were those who, like Elmer, Brigid, and Seamus, accepted him for who he was, leprechaun or not. They stood by him,
offering their support and friendship without hesitation. They
had made it clear, in their own quiet ways, that Finn's identity
didn't change how they saw him. **He was still Finn. He was still
one of them.**

Elmer, ever the optimist, had gone out of his way to make sure
Finn didn't feel like an outcast. "We're a team, remember?"
he'd said, grinning and giving Finn a light punch on the arm.
"Doesn't matter if you're a leprechaun or an elf. You've got
our backs, and we've got yours." The sincerity in his voice had
been enough to bring a small, grateful smile to Finn's face.

Brigid had been just as supportive in her quiet way. She had
stayed close, offering her calming presence without needing
to say much. When Finn had stumbled over words trying to explain himself, she had simply squeezed his shoulder and said,
"It's alright, Finn. We all make mistakes."

Even Seamus had found a way to turn the situation into something lighthearted. "Hey, now we've got a leprechaun on the
team. That's got to be good luck, right?" he'd said with a wink.
Finn had chuckled despite himself, appreciating Seamus's ability to find humor even in the most awkward moments.

But not everyone was so understanding.

Nessa Goldenbloom had been colder than ever. She hadn't spoken to him since the news broke, but her disdain was palpable. Whenever they crossed paths, she would fix him with a glare so sharp it made Finn's stomach twist with unease. Her eyes, once merely critical, now held a kind of silent judgment that cut deeper than any words.

"A leprechaun," she had muttered to a group of recruits, her voice dripping with contempt. "I knew there was something off about him. Deceiving us all like that... It's disgraceful."

The words had stung, but Finn had forced himself to hold his head high. He couldn't change her opinion, no matter how hard he tried.

And then, of course, there was **Kieran Shadowbrook**.

Kieran had been the hardest to face. After their confrontation the night before, Kieran had made it clear that forgiveness wouldn't come easily—if it came at all. He hadn't spoken a word to Finn since then, and every time their paths crossed, Kieran's eyes were cold, his expression closed off. There was a distance between them now, like a wall that Finn wasn't sure he could break through.

It weighed heavily on him. **Kieran had trusted him once.** They had worked side by side, trained together, fought through challenges as a team. But now that trust was shattered, and Finn knew it would take more than words to rebuild it.

But Finn wasn't ready to give up. He had been given a second chance by the council—and he was determined to earn a second chance with his team.

Merry
Christmas

That evening, after a long day of training, Finn found Kieran sitting alone in the courtyard. The snow was falling softly, blanketing the ground in a thin, white layer. The air was crisp, and the courtyard was quiet, save for the occasional whistle of the wind and the faint laughter of recruits coming from inside the school.

Finn hesitated as he stood at the edge of the courtyard, watching Kieran's solitary figure. His teammate sat on a stone bench, staring out at the snow with his arms crossed over his chest, his expression unreadable. The silence between them was thick, the weight of unspoken words hanging in the air.

Is this a good idea? Finn thought, doubt creeping in. Kieran had made it clear that he wasn't ready to forgive him. Maybe it was better to leave things as they were. Maybe trying to talk now would only make things worse.

But he couldn't keep avoiding this. **He had to try.**

Taking a deep breath, Finn squared his shoulders and walked over, his boots crunching softly in the snow.

"Kieran?"

Kieran didn't look up, didn't acknowledge him at first. He just kept staring ahead, his jaw tight. "What do you want, Finn?"

The coldness in Kieran's voice made Finn flinch. **He had expected it, but that didn't make it any easier to hear.** Finn swallowed, trying to steady his nerves.

"I just... I wanted to talk," Finn began, his voice quieter than he'd intended. "I know you're angry, and you have every right to be. But I need you to know that I'm sorry. I never meant to hurt you—or anyone else."

At that, Kieran finally looked up, his eyes dark and guarded. "Sorry?" he repeated, his tone flat. "You think an apology fixes everything?"

Finn shook his head quickly, his heart racing. "No. I don't. I know I messed up. I know I lied, and I know I broke your trust. But I didn't lie because I didn't care. I lied because... because I was scared."

Kieran's brow furrowed slightly, the first crack in his cold demeanor. "Scared?" he echoed, his voice edged with skepticism.

Finn nodded, his throat tight. **This was his chance to be honest—to lay everything out.** "I didn't think I could ever belong here," he admitted, the words heavy with the weight of his own fear. "I'm not like you. I'm not like any of the other recruits. I'm a leprechaun—my whole life has been about guarding gold and pulling pranks. But I wanted more than that. I wanted to be part of something bigger, something meaningful. So, I lied. I thought... I thought if I could just prove myself, maybe I'd belong here."

Kieran's eyes remained on him, unreadable, but he didn't interrupt. Finn pressed on, his voice quieter now. "I didn't mean to hurt anyone. I just wanted a chance to be more than what I was."

The silence that followed was almost unbearable. Finn stood there, his heart pounding in his chest, waiting for Kieran's response. The snowfall seemed to slow, the world around them pausing as if holding its breath. **Had he said enough? Would Kieran understand?**

Finally, Kieran sighed, running a hand through his dark hair. "Look, Finn," he said, his voice still tense but less harsh. "I get it. You wanted a chance. But you didn't just lie to the school—you lied to us. To me. And that's... that's not something I can just forget."

Finn felt a pang of guilt, his chest tightening. **Kieran was right.** He had betrayed their trust. There was no denying that. "I know," Finn said softly, his voice barely more than a whisper. "And I'll do whatever it takes to earn your trust back. I just hope... I hope you'll give me the chance to."

Kieran was silent for a long moment, his gaze drifting back to the snow-covered ground. His expression was still guarded, but there was something softer in his eyes now—something that hadn't been there before.

"I don't know, Finn," Kieran said finally, his voice quiet. "Maybe... maybe we can start over. But it's going to take time."

Finn felt a flicker of hope, small but warm in the cold night air. **It wasn't a complete forgiveness**—not yet—but it was something. It was more than he had expected.

"I understand," Finn said, his voice steady but full of gratitude. "Thank you."

Kieran didn't respond, but he gave a small nod, his eyes still focused on the snow. It wasn't much, but it was a step. **A small step forward.**

As Finn turned to leave, he felt lighter, the weight of their unresolved tension beginning to ease, if only just a little. It wasn't perfect, but it was a start—and for now, that was enough.

Chapter 17: The Final Challenge

The weeks passed, and slowly, Finn began to rebuild trust with his teammates.

It wasn't easy. The scars of his deception still lingered, surfacing in awkward moments, lingering doubts, and the occasional tense exchange. Some days, it felt like things were almost back to normal—like the weight of the past was finally lifting. Other days, it felt

like he was walking on thin ice, never quite sure if it would hold or crack beneath him. But bit by bit, the fractures in Team Donner began to heal.

Elmer had been the glue, always quick to joke and keep the mood light. Brigid, with her quiet strength, had been a steady presence, never letting the tension linger too long. Even Seamus, with his endless humor, had helped ease the rough edges. **But Kieran and Nessa?** They were different stories.

Kieran was thawing—slowly. Their conversations were less guarded now, and sometimes, Finn would catch a glimpse of the old camaraderie they'd once had. But it wasn't fully repaired. Trust wasn't something you rebuilt overnight, and Finn knew that. **He would keep trying.**

Nessa, though, was another matter. She had been the most vocal about her anger when the truth came out, and while she had cooled somewhat, there was still a distance between them. She didn't snap at him anymore, but her silence around him was thick with unspoken judgments. Her icy looks told Finn everything he needed to know. **She wasn't ready to forgive.** Maybe she never would.

But Finn didn't push her. He knew better. Some wounds took longer to heal than others, and Nessa's pride had been deeply wounded by his deception. Still, he couldn't help but hope that time might soften her heart, the way it had slowly started to with Kieran.

As Christmas Eve approached, the school buzzed with excitement. The day everyone had been training for—the night of **Santa's Annual Sleigh Flight**—was nearly upon them. And with it came the final test for the recruits: the task that would determine who would earn the honor of joining Santa's crew for the big night.

This was it.

It was a tradition as old as the school itself. Every year, the top-performing recruits were chosen to assist in Santa's sleigh preparation—a role that carried both immense honor and responsibility. For many, it was the pinnacle of their training, a chance to prove themselves worthy of being part of Santa's elite crew.

Finn had dreamed about this moment since he first arrived at the school, but now that it was here, the pressure felt immense. **This was his last chance.** Not just to prove himself capable, but to show that he had truly earned his place among the team. **He had to show them that he belonged here—not just as a recruit, but as their equal.**

But the final challenge was no ordinary test.

Master Evergreen gathered the recruits in the grand courtyard, his voice carrying through the crisp winter air as he explained the task. The courtyard had been transformed into a sparkling winter wonderland, with snow gently falling around them and lanterns casting soft, golden light across the gleaming stone.

"This year's final challenge will test not just your skills, but your heart," Master Evergreen announced, his sharp gaze sweeping over the group. His voice was firm but with an underlying warmth that made every recruit straighten with anticipation. "It will require more than strength or speed. You will need to work together, trust one another, and show the true spirit of Christmas."

Finn's stomach fluttered with nerves, a familiar knot tightening in his chest. He had been working so hard to prove himself, but this final challenge felt like **the ultimate test**—not just of his abilities, but of the fragile trust he had been trying to rebuild with his team.

"The task is simple in concept," Master Evergreen continued, "but the journey will not be easy. Your team must navigate the Frozen Forest and retrieve a magical snowflake from the heart of the Ice Palace. Each team will be given a special compass to guide them, but the path is treacherous. The forest is enchanted and will test you at every turn."

Finn felt his breath catch in his throat. **The Frozen Forest.** He had heard about it in whispers and tales. The forest was notorious for its shifting paths, its illusions, and the strange creatures that roamed its icy depths. Few ventured into it, and even fewer returned without facing significant challenges.

Master Evergreen's voice softened, yet carried more weight as he spoke. "The team that retrieves the snowflake first will earn the honor of assisting Santa's sleigh team on Christmas Eve.

But remember—this test is not just about speed. It is about showing who you are as a team. The Frozen Forest will reveal your strengths... and your weaknesses."

A heavy silence fell over the recruits as they absorbed the weight of his words. Finn's heart raced. This wasn't just a challenge; it was a test of everything they had learned, everything they had worked for. **It was their last chance to prove themselves.**

Master Evergreen gave them a small, knowing smile. "Good luck," he said simply, and with that, the final challenge was set.

As the teams gathered to receive their compasses, Finn exchanged a glance with his teammates. There was a mix of excitement and nervousness in their eyes, but something else too—**determination.**

They had come so far together, had weathered so many storms. This was their moment to prove they had healed, that they were stronger as a team. Finn felt it in the way they stood shoulder to shoulder, no longer distant or divided. **They were in this together.**

Elmer grinned at him, his bright eyes full of optimism. "Alright, Team Donner," he said, his voice bubbling with excitement. "Let's go get that snowflake!"

Brigid smiled softly, her calm presence a steadying force. "We've made it this far," she said, her voice low but full of quiet confidence. "We can do this."

Even Kieran, who had been distant for so long, gave a small nod, his expression serious but resolute. "Let's just make sure we stick together," he said, his voice measured. There was no hint of hesitation, no lingering distrust—just the understanding that they were a team. And teams stuck together.

Finn felt a surge of gratitude well up inside him, his heart swelling with pride. For the first time in what felt like forever, he truly believed that they could do this. Not just because they were strong or fast, but because they had learned to trust one another again.

He had spent so long trying to prove he belonged here. Now, standing beside his team, he realized that belonging wasn't something you proved. It was something you earned through the bonds you forged, through trust and resilience.

Together.

"Let's do it," Finn said, his voice steady, his gaze fixed on the snowy path ahead. And as they set off into the Frozen Forest, the weight of the past weeks began to lift, replaced by something stronger. **Hope.**

Chapter 18: The Frozen Forest

The **Frozen Forest** was even more daunting than Finn had imagined.

The moment they stepped beneath the towering, ice-laden trees, it was as if they had entered another world—**a world that didn't want them there.**

The temperature dropped instantly, the chill biting through their heavy coats and sinking deep into their bones. **The cold**

wasn't natural. It was sharper, more intense, as though the forest itself was drawing heat from their bodies, testing their endurance. Finn shivered, pulling his collar up around his neck, but it did little to fend off the numbing frost.

The trees loomed overhead, their dark branches intertwined like twisted fingers, coated in glittering layers of ice that shimmered like glass. The ground was blanketed in a thick layer of snow, untouched and pure, as if no one had ventured this way in years. The air was eerily still—**too still**—and the silence pressed down on them, heavy and unnatural, like the forest was holding its breath.

In Elmer's hand, the enchanted compass glowed faintly, the needle pointing the way forward. It was their only guide through the shifting, enchanted paths, but even with it, the way ahead felt uncertain—**treacherous.**

"Stay close," Brigid whispered, her eyes scanning the trees with quiet caution. "This place... it feels alive."

Finn nodded, his heart pounding in his chest. He felt it too. The air hummed with a strange energy, a magic that made the hairs on the back of his neck stand on end. **It was as if the forest was watching them, waiting, testing their every move.**

They moved cautiously, the soft crunch of their boots in the snow the only sound breaking the eerie silence. The compass's needle glowed steadily, pointing them deeper into the heart of the forest, but the path itself was anything but steady.

The trees seemed to shift around them, the landscape twisting in subtle, almost imperceptible ways. Sometimes the path would stretch impossibly long, and at other moments, it felt like they hadn't moved at all. **The forest played tricks with their senses, twisting time and space until forward and backward blurred together.**

"We need to trust the compass," Kieran said, his voice steady but laced with tension. "It's the only thing that won't deceive us."

Finn swallowed, glancing at his teammates. They were all feeling it—the sense of disorientation, the creeping unease. He could see it in the way Elmer's hands gripped the compass just a little too tightly, in the flicker of doubt in Brigid's usually calm eyes.

The deeper they ventured, the more the forest began to reveal its true nature.

At first, it was subtle—a soft whisper in the wind that almost sounded like voices, fleeting shadows at the edges of their vision that disappeared the moment they turned to look. **But soon, the illusions grew bolder.**

One moment, they were walking on solid ground, the snow crunching beneath their boots. The next, the earth beneath them cracked open without warning, revealing a gaping chasm. Finn's breath caught in his throat as the ground trembled beneath him, the abyss widening at his feet. Instinctively, he grabbed Elmer's arm, yanking him back just in time.

"Wait!" Finn shouted, his heart hammering in his chest. **But then—just as quickly as it had appeared—the chasm vanished.**

The ground was solid again, undisturbed snow blanketing the

earth as if nothing had happened.

"This place is messing with us," Kieran muttered, his jaw tight, his eyes scanning the trees with suspicion. "We can't trust what we see."

Finn's pulse raced. **If they couldn't trust their own eyes, how could they possibly make it through?**

But it wasn't just the illusions. As they pressed forward, a low growl rumbled through the forest, the sound vibrating in the still air. It was deep, primal—**and close.** The snow beneath their feet seemed to tremble with it. Finn's blood ran cold as the sound of heavy, deliberate footsteps followed, crunching through the snow from somewhere just beyond the trees.

Shadows shifted, and out of the darkness stepped a **creature made of ice and snow**, its massive form towering over them, its eyes glowing like embers in the night.

Finn's breath caught in his throat, his body frozen with fear as the creature stalked toward them, each step slow and deliberate, its breath curling in the frigid air like smoke. **It looked like it had been carved from the forest itself.** Ice crusted its massive limbs, and jagged spikes of frozen snow jutted from its shoulders, glittering in the dim light.

Finn could feel the fear tightening around his team like a noose, their breaths coming in shallow, visible puffs.

"What do we do?" Elmer whispered, his voice trembling.

Finn didn't know. His heart pounded so loudly in his chest, he could barely think. But in the stillness, something inside him stirred—something fierce, something that refused to let fear take over.

"We stand together," Finn said, his voice louder than he expected. He stepped forward before he could second-guess himself, his pulse roaring in his ears. "We don't run. Not this time."

The creature snarled, its eyes flickering with cold fire. But as Finn stood firm, the beast hesitated, its glowing eyes narrowing.

"It's testing us," Finn realized, his breath visible in the frozen air. "It's trying to see if we'll break."

He could feel it now, the magic of the forest—the way it probed their weaknesses, the way it whispered doubts into their minds. **But if they could stand together, they could make it through.**

They pressed deeper into the forest, following the compass's glowing needle, but the forest wasn't finished with them yet.

As they approached the Ice Palace, the creatures became more frequent. **Snow wraiths** hovered at the edges of the trees, ghostly figures made of swirling ice and snow. Their glowing eyes watched the team with cold, silent hunger, their ethereal forms flickering in and out of view like shadows on the wind.

"We need to keep moving," Brigid whispered, her voice taut with fear. "We can't let them get too close."

The wraiths didn't attack, but their presence was suffocating. Their cold gazes followed every step, and the air seemed to grow colder with each passing minute, sapping the strength from their bodies.

"We're close," Elmer said, his voice strained. His eyes were fixed on the compass, its glow brighter now. "The Ice Palace should be just ahead."

But just as hope flickered to life, the ground beneath them shifted again—**this time, for real.**

Without warning, a crack split the ice beneath Finn's feet. His heart lurched as the world seemed to drop away. The ice gave way, and before Finn could react, he was falling—tumbling into the dark, icy abyss below.

"Finn!" Kieran's voice echoed through the forest, but it was too late.

Finn hit the ground hard, the impact knocking the air from his lungs. Pain shot through his body, sharp and relentless. For a moment, he couldn't move, couldn't breathe. **Just the cold— the bitter, biting cold—seeping into his bones.**

He lay there, gasping, trying to gather his bearings. Above him, he could hear his teammates calling his name, their voices filled with panic and fear. "Finn! Are you okay?"

"I'm fine," Finn called back, though every inch of his body ached. "Just... just give me a minute."

As he tried to stand, something caught his eye—a faint glow, pulsing softly from the ice beneath him.

Curiosity piqued, Finn brushed away the snow, revealing a small, glowing snowflake embedded in the ice. His breath caught in his throat.

It was the magical snowflake. The one they had been sent to retrieve.

For a moment, all the pain, all the fear, seemed to melt away. **This was it.** The very thing they had come for—right here, glowing softly in his hands.

But now, he had to get back to his team.

"Finn!" Kieran's voice was closer now, echoing down into the crevasse. "Can you climb out?"

Finn looked up at the sheer walls of ice surrounding him. It would be a painful climb, but he had to try. "I'll need some help," he called back.

Moments later, a rope was lowered down to him, and with his teammates' help, Finn began the slow, grueling ascent. His muscles screamed with effort, and the cold bit at his fingers, but **he refused to give up.**

When he finally reached the top, Elmer and Brigid pulled him to his feet, their faces full of relief.

"You found it," Brigid breathed, her eyes wide as she saw the glowing snowflake in Finn's hand.

Finn nodded, his chest swelling with pride despite the pain radiating through his body. "We did it."

They had braved the forest, faced its illusions, its creatures, its tricks—and they had won. **Together.**

Chapter 19: A Place to Belong

By the time **Team Donner** returned to the school, the other teams were already gathering in the courtyard, their faces alight with excitement and anticipation. The courtyard itself seemed to glow in the evening light, the soft shimmer of snow reflecting the warm golden hues from the lanterns overhead. The air was crisp, the chill biting at Finn's skin, but it wasn't the cold that made his breath catch in his throat—it was the weight of the moment.

In the center of the courtyard, **Master Evergreen** stood tall, his sharp eyes scanning the returning recruits. In his hands, the magical snowflake shimmered faintly, casting soft sparkles of light across the snow dusted ground. Finn's heart raced, his breath visible in the frosty air, but for the first time in what felt like months, his mind was still. **He felt a sense of calm he hadn't known he could reach.** This moment wasn't just a culmination of the tests they had faced—it was the end of a journey he had once thought impossible.

Master Evergreen's gaze swept over **Team Donner**, and for a moment, his eyes lingered on Finn. **The rare smile** that crept onto the instructor's face sent a wave of warmth through Finn's chest. The approving nod that followed wasn't just for the team—it felt personal. Like recognition. **Like validation.**

"Well done, Team Donner," Master Evergreen announced, his voice ringing out across the courtyard. "You have passed the final test."

The applause erupted almost instantly, the other recruits cheering, their voices echoing off the frosted stone walls.

Merry
Christmas

The sound filled the courtyard, swelling around Finn like a tidal wave of relief and pride. His chest swelled as he glanced around at his teammates—**Elmer, Brigid, Kieran, and even Nessa.** Each of them looked different than they had months ago, each battle hardened in their own way. But it wasn't just the challenges that had changed them. **It was the way they had come together.**

He locked eyes with Nessa across the crowd. She gave him a small, grudging nod, a silent acknowledgment that held more weight than any words. Nessa had been the hardest to win over, and while their relationship would likely never be easy, there was respect now. **That was enough.**

Finn's fingers brushed the magical snowflake as Master Evergreen passed it off to **Santa's sleigh crew**, and for a moment, he just stared at it—the soft glow, the faint warmth radiating from within. It wasn't just a symbol of the magic they had been sent to retrieve—it was a reminder of how far he had come. **How far they had all come.**

This wasn't just a victory. It was the culmination of everything he had fought for. He had spent so long trying to prove that he could belong—that he could be more than just a trickster leprechaun, more than the mischief-maker everyone expected him to be. Now, standing with his team, Finn knew he had done more than just prove it to others. **He had proved it to himself.**

He wasn't just a leprechaun. He wasn't just a boy who guarded a pot of gold and played tricks. He was **Finn O'Malley**, a member of **Team Donner**, and he had earned his place here.

As the celebration continued, laughter and cheers filling the cold winter air, Finn felt a hand rest gently on his shoulder. He turned to find **Kieran** standing beside him, a tentative smile tugging at his lips.

"You did good, Finn," Kieran said, his voice quiet but sincere. There was something in his tone—something Finn hadn't heard from him before. **Respect.**

For a long time, Kieran had been the hardest to read. They had clashed from the beginning, their differences often leading to arguments and mistrust. But looking back, Finn could see that Kieran's challenges hadn't been born out of arrogance or disdain. **Kieran had pushed him because he wanted them all to be better.** It hadn't always felt that way, but now, Finn understood.

Finn hesitated for a moment, then smiled back. "We all did," he said, the weight of everything that had passed between them lifting like a fog. The rivalry, the misunderstandings, the moments of frustration—they had led them here, to this shared victory. **Together.**

Kieran's eyes softened, and the tension between them that had lingered for so long seemed to dissolve in the cold evening air. The friction that had once driven them apart now felt like something they had both outgrown, something that had forged a deeper understanding between them. "Yeah," Kieran nodded. "We did."

The relief that washed over Finn was almost overwhelming. **This wasn't just a personal victory—it was a team victory.** And for the first time, Finn felt like he wasn't just part of the team—**he was truly part of the family.**

As the night wore on, the celebration in the courtyard grew more jubilant. Music filled the air, the tinkling of bells and the soft hum of Christmas carols weaving through the crowd. Finn watched as the sleigh crew prepared Santa's reindeer, the soft jingling of their harness bells adding to the festive atmosphere. There was a kind of magic in the air that night—**not the kind of magic you could cast with a spell, but something deeper.**

It was the magic of shared effort, of triumph after struggle, of friendships forged through hardship. It was the kind of magic that made Finn feel grounded, connected to something much bigger than himself. The snowflake had been the task, the challenge—but the real reward was the bond he had formed with his teammates, the trust they had built together.

As the first stars appeared in the clear winter sky, **Santa's sleigh lifted off into the night.** The reindeer's hooves skimmed across the snow before they soared higher, disappearing into the sky, the faint jingle of their bells fading into the distance.

Finn stood with his team, his heart full, watching as the sleigh disappeared into the stars. For the first time in his life, he knew with absolute certainty that he belonged. Not just to Team Donner, but to something bigger—**something magical, something real.**

And it wasn't just because of the magic in the air, or the snowflake they had retrieved, or the honor of being part of this school. It was because of the bonds they had forged, the battles they had fought, and the trust they had built. Whatever challenges came next, Finn knew they would face them together.

Epilogue: A Bright Future

Christmas morning dawned bright and clear, the snow sparkling under the soft light of the rising sun. The courtyard, now quiet and still, held the lingering echoes of the previous night's celebration. **Everything had changed, but in the most peaceful way.**

Finn sat on a small hill overlooking the school, the crisp air filling his lungs as he gazed out over the snow-covered landscape. **This place had become his home.**

The past few months had been a whirlwind—filled with challenges, mistakes, lessons learned, and triumphs earned. But it wasn't just the victories that stuck with him. It was the moments of doubt, the times when he'd thought he would never fit in—when he had been sure he was destined to always be on the outside, looking in.

But those moments were behind him now. They didn't haunt him anymore. **They were part of his journey, but they didn't define him.**

As he watched the sun rise, casting golden light over the snow, Finn knew that the journey wasn't over. Far from it. There would be new challenges ahead—maybe even bigger ones—but for the first time, he wasn't afraid. **He had his team. He had his place.**

More than that, he had a future to look forward to.

And as he sat there, the quiet of the morning settling around him, Finn couldn't help but smile. The snow sparkled beneath the rising sun, the warmth of his own breath curling softly into the cold air, and Finn felt something he hadn't felt in a long time.

Peace.

He had found where he belonged. And wherever life took him next, he knew he would meet it head-on—with his friends, his family, and his newfound confidence by his side.

The End

Merry
Christmas

About Me

I was born in Scotland and have lived here all my life. For thirty years, I worked in the North Sea for Marathon Oil, a unique and amazing environment that always reminded me of how special the world is. During my time at sea, I would make up stories for my two boys, spinning wild tales about the places I had been. One of their favourites was the story about six-foot-tall seagulls with attitude!

I've always been a dreamer, and my first love was art. I am self-taught in digital art techniques and love using computers to create various pieces of artwork. My vivid imagination and creative spirit continue to inspire my storytelling today.